HARLEQUIN® Presents

Great news! From this month onward, Harlequin Presents® is offering you more!

Now, when you go to your local bookstore, you'll find that you have *eight* Harlequin Presents® titles to choose from—more of your favorite authors, more of the stories you love.

To help you make your selection from our July books, here are the fabulous titles that are available: *Prince of the Desert* by Penny Jordan—hot desert nights! *The Scorsolini Marriage Bargain* by Lucy Monroe—the final part of an unforgettable royal trilogy! *Naked in His Arms* by Sandra Marton— the third Knight Brothers story and a sensationally sensual read to boot! *The Secret Baby Revenge* by Emma Darcy—a passionate Latin lover and a shocking secret from his past! *At the Greek Tycoon's Bidding* by Cathy Williams—an ordinary girl and the most gorgeous Greek millionaire! *The Italian's Convenient Wife* by Catherine Spencer—passion, tears and joy as a marriage is announced! *The Jet-Set Seduction* by Sandra Field—fasten your seat belt and prepare to be whisked away to glamorous foreign locations! *Mistress on Demand* by Maggie Cox—he's rich, ruthless and really...irresistible!

Remember, in July, Harlequin Presents® promises more reading pleasure. Enjoy!

Emma Darcy

THE SECRET BABY REVENGE

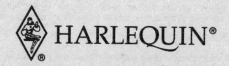

HARLEQUIN®

TORONTO • NEW YORK • LONDON
AMSTERDAM • PARIS • SYDNEY • HAMBURG
STOCKHOLM • ATHENS • TOKYO • MILAN • MADRID
PRAGUE • WARSAW • BUDAPEST • AUCKLAND

ISBN-13: 978-0-373-23314-4
ISBN-10:   0-373-23314-0

THE SECRET BABY REVENGE

First North American Publication 2006.

Copyright © 2006 by Emma Darcy.

This edition published by arrangement with Harlequin Books S.A.

www.eHarlequin.com

Printed in U.S.A.

All about the author…
Emma Darcy

EMMA DARCY was born in Australia, and currently lives on a beautiful country property in New South Wales. Her ambition to be an actress was partly satisfied by playing in amateur theater productions, but ultimately fulfilled in becoming a writer, where she has the exciting pleasure of playing all the roles!

Initially a teacher of French and English, she changed her career to computer programming before marriage and motherhood settled her into a community life. Her creative urges were channeled into oil painting, pottery, designing and overseeing the construction and decorating of two homes, all in the midst of keeping up with three lively sons and the very busy social life of her businessman husband.

A voracious reader, the step to writing her own books seemed natural and the challenge of creating wonderful stories was soon highly addictive. With her strong interest in people and relationships, Emma found the world of romance fiction a happy one. Currently, she has broadened her horizons and begun to write mainstream women's fiction.

Her conviction that we must make all we can out of the life we are given keeps her striving to know more, be more and give more—this is reflected in all her books.

CHAPTER ONE

OPENING night at Sydney's new Havana Club and Joaquin Luis Sola stood at the extremely busy bar, waiting for the drinks he'd ordered and idly watching the talent on the dance floor swirl by. His friend, legal advisor, and highly eligible man about town, Tony Fisher, had promised all the *beautiful* people would be here, to see and be seen in the hotspot of the moment, and Quin could undoubtedly pick himself a partner for more than dancing.

Much waggling of eyebrows to underline the point, but for Quin, joining Tony's party was more an escape from a sense of restless boredom than a quest for casual sex. Having recently ended a less than satisfying relationship, Quin wasn't sure he wanted to complicate his life with another woman just yet. A one-night stand didn't appeal, either. He wasn't actually watching for targets of possible interest, just watching…

A colourful kaleidoscope of couples were swinging around the dance floor, doing the salsa. Latin American dancing was big on the social scene right now due to a number of popular television shows featuring competitions. The Havana Club was cleverly capitalising on this latest trend.

"Great way of meeting people," Tony had enthused. "Everyone putting themselves on display, strutting their stuff."

They were certainly doing that, Quin thought, somewhat bemused by the exuberant and very public plunge into fun and fantasy. Most of the people here had wildly embraced Latin dance fashion; the guys in fitted shirts with big cuffs, bootleg pants, much attention paid to their hairdos; the women very glamorous in slinky sheaths with side splits, skintight black pants with halter midriff tops, frilled skirts and strappy stilettos.

Being in this club was like being in an exotic and erotic foreign country. Quin could see its appeal—a quick fix escape from the pressures of today's fast and frantic society— a place where people could let their hair down, revel in uninhibited dress-ups, enjoy the primitive pleasure of moving to music, not to mention the sexual excitement…with the right partner.

A flashy couple caught his eye. The guy was all in white, his long black hair slicked back into a ponytail—very dramatic with his dark olive skin and hard featured handsome face. The woman partnering him was wearing a virtually backless black dress, its figure-hugging skirt ending in a ruffle edged in white. She also had long black hair, but it was a wild loose mass of curls falling to below her shoulder-blades, reminding Quin instantly of Nicole Ashton—not a memory he cared to dwell on.

"Your drinks, sir?"

Quin paid the bartender, cynically reflecting that the price of cocktails in this club belonged to the fantasy realm, too, aimed at a clientele who never counted the cost. Strange how it didn't matter how wealthy he had become, the concept of value for money still counted in his mind. Not that it stopped him from doing or buying whatever he wanted. It was simply impossible to forget the lessons of poverty.

With the drinks firmly clutched in his

hands, Quin turned to weave his way around the crowded dance floor to the tables Tony had claimed for his party, and found the woman with Nicole's hair twirling right in front of him.

She had a great body; lush breasts straining against a halter-necked bodice edged in white. The skirt was split up to midthigh, the ruffle following the opening up, diminishing to a white tie-belt around a hand-span waist. Her hips were female poetry and her long shapely legs flashed with sexy elegance.

The guy in white caught her and dipped her over his knee, her lovely lithe body arched, toes in their black stilettos pointed, head thrown back, hair sweeping the floor, stunning green eyes sparkling with pleasure, her whole beautiful face vividly lit by a laughing smile—a face that delivered such a jolt to Quin, the drinks he was carrying sloshed over the rims of the glasses.

It *was* Nicole!

The thump to his heart and the kick to his gut were instantaneous. Shock, he tried to reason, after he'd pulled himself back from shooting a blistering bolt of hatred at the guy in white and halted the rampant urge to tear Nicole away from him.

Quite simply hadn't expected to run into her like this, hadn't expected their paths ever to cross again. She'd gone overseas after breaking up with him, taking herself completely out of his reach, yet here she was in this Sussex Street club, right under his nose. And attached to another guy.

Which also stood to reason, Quin savagely told himself. Why wouldn't she move on to other men? He'd moved on to other women, though never feeling the same intensity Nicole had drawn from him. In fact, he hadn't wanted to feel any deep emotional connection with anyone after *she* had walked out of his life. It was easier to function on the fast-moving business level without that kind of distraction.

And it was totally absurd to get in a twist over Nicole now. What was gone was gone. He wrenched his gaze away from the dance floor and guarded the drinks in his hands as he made his way back to those in Tony's party who were sitting out this number. He sat down next to Amber Piramo who'd requested the liquid refreshment, expecting him to pay and deliver, expecting her every whim to be indulged because she was the beautiful socialite daughter of old-wealth parents.

"Oh, thank you, my darling Quin," she gushed. "I am totally, totally dehydrated."

He wasn't her darling, and despite her obvious physical attractions, the overly flirtatious manner grated on him. He had to force a smile as he responded, "Sorry I was so long at the bar."

"No problem." She patted his thigh as she added, "It's been fun just watching the other dancers."

His leg muscles tensed, instinctively repelling the touch. His jaw clenched, too. The only touch he wanted…but Nicole was with someone else now.

Amber withdrew the inviting hand and wrapped it around her glass. She drank too much, too fast, revealing a reckless disregard for the alcoholic content of the cocktail. Quin hoped she wasn't working up some courage to be more direct in coming onto him. While it might be an old-fashioned attitude these days, he still felt it was a man's prerogative to be the hunter.

His gaze instinctively targeted Nicole as the music stopped. Her ponytailed partner swept her to a table where another guy had just left a woman with wildly purple hair—definitely not a shrinking violet, wearing a black midriff top and skintight hot-pink pants. Intriguingly the three of them cosied up together, chatting and laughing—two women, one man between them, all very friendly.

Quin's view of them was blocked by Tony, comically miming wobbly legs and wiping his brow as he escorted his latest *amour,* Nina Salter-Smythe off the dance floor. "I need a fast and long injection of cold beer," he declared, leaving Nina at the table while he headed for the bar. She suggested a visit to the powder room to Amber and the two women went off together, leaving Quin free to watch Nicole without interruption.

He tried reminding himself this was a woman who had rejected him. He shouldn't be giving her a second thought, let alone a second look. It was an exercise in futility, in frustration.

Yet all his aggressive instincts were on fire. She'd been *his* woman and he wanted another chance with her. If she wasn't actually married to the Latin lover who was flashing his eyes at both women indiscriminately, he had room to move.

And move he would.

His whole body was screaming at him to

do it, mount an attack, get Nicole back into his life.

The moment Tony returned to the table, ready to play jovial host to the rest of his party friends, Quin was on his feet to intercept him before he sat down. "Spotted someone I want to meet," he explained. "Excuse me, won't you?"

"Wait a sec," came the quick protest. "How goes it with Amber? She's been eyeing you over."

"Non-event," Quin almost snapped, raising his hand to ward off any further comment as he swung to make a beeline for the woman who was *the only event* in his mind tonight.

CHAPTER TWO

NICOLE was having fun. She was glad she'd let Jade and Jules talk her into accompanying them here tonight. They had argued she should be armed with a firsthand report of the new Havana Club to pass onto her pupils, unaware that the dance school she was managing for her mother was in such dire debt that Nicole couldn't see a way out of it. She had accepted their invitation in a desperate need to push her worries aside for a while, to simply enjoy the zany company of her friends and not think about facing tomorrow until it came.

"Handsome hunk zeroing in on you, Nic." Jade rolled her big brown eyes expressively. "To your left. Nine o'clock."

Nicole laughed. "Score out of ten?"

"Ten plus."

She shook her head disbelievingly. Ever

since Jade had returned from her extensive work experience with designers in Europe to set up business in Sydney, she had been trying to *fix* Nicole up with some guy, preaching one should keep involved with everything life had to offer, seeing Nicole's single status as unhealthy, even stunting her growth as a woman.

Jules leaned over and whispered in her ear, "Got to say Jade's spot-on. Mega macho bearing down on you. A star player."

Nicole winced at that phrase. Jules wouldn't know it—not his field—but it was the phrase used in banking circles to describe the top guns on the trading floor, and she'd once been intimately attached to *a star player*. Attached and burnt.

"Nicole…"

That voice…a convulsive little shiver instantly ran down her spine. Her skin went cold. Her stomach contracted as her head jerked around, reacting to the need to deny the recognition blasting her mind and thumping into her heart. Except the recognition was not a mad mistake.

"Quin…" His name fell from her lips before she could catch it back, and the awful part was the lingering sound of it seemed to carry a longing that was intensely embarrassing. She should have been expressing surprise.

It was certainly that.

He smiled, hitting her with the same megawatt attraction that had been her downfall seven years ago, his bullet grey eyes cutting straight through all lines of defence. The only thing that had changed about him were the silver threads shining through his thick thatch of black hair, giving a more mature authority to his strikingly handsome face—a face which had never lacked authority with its sharply chiselled features adding male strength and character to it. His tall, powerful physique shouted strength, as well, not to mention compelling sex appeal.

"Good to see you again, Nicole," he rolled out, the smooth deep timbre of his voice raising goose-bumps.

"What are you doing here?" The words burst abruptly from a surge of resentment at the way he could still affect her. He had dominated her life for two years—two years that had ultimately taught her she was nothing more than a sexual convenience to him.

His smile wasn't even slightly shaken. "I enjoy dancing…remember?"

She didn't want to remember *anything*. Though he had been a great dancer the few times it actually suited him to partner her at parties.

"Hi! I'm Jade Zilic." Typical Jade, too fascinated to wait for an introduction, hand thrust out in ready friendship. "And you are?"

"Joaquin Sola. Mostly called Quin." He took her hand, nodding a polite acknowledgment, looking enquiringly at Jules.

"My partner, Jules," Jade obliged, leaving Nicole exposed as partnerless tonight.

Jules thrust out his hand and it was promptly taken and shaken with vigour. "Pleased to meet you both," Quin said, warm pleasure positively emanating from him.

Field clear, Nicole bitterly interpreted, though second thoughts zipped into her mind. Quin could not be here womanless. A man like him didn't have to go anywhere alone and he wouldn't to a club. No doubt he had some banking clique with him, having a night on the town.

"I have one question for you," Jade shot at him, her eyes dancing wicked mischief.

"Yes?" he invited.

"Are you wearing *Nick's Knickers?*"

The charming smile definitely faltered at that point, his gaze swinging to Nicole, furrowed brow indicating fast reassessment of the situation. Did the somewhat bawdy question relate to knowledge of his being Nicole's former lover? Was he being cast as a bunny here? Someone to make fun of?

Nicole quite enjoyed seeing the brilliant Joaquin Sola lost for a moment. It made her feel slightly less vulnerable. Though when his thick black eyelashes lowered and a steamy look smoked through them at her, suggesting his thoughts had fastened on her knickers, she rushed out an explanation of the question.

"It's a new range of male underwear, designed and promoted by my friends here."

A deeper frown as his gaze sliced back to her friends. "*Business* partners?"

"Uh-huh. With very hot merchandise," Jules advised with a wide grin.

"Guaranteed to bring out the devil in a man," Jade backed up, then heaved a dramatic sigh of woe. "The advertising campaign can't be working as effectively as it should if Quin hasn't even caught onto the brand name."

"Don't judge by *his* ignorance," Nicole dryly commented. "Quin doesn't have the time nor the inclination to watch commercial television."

"Really?" Jade eyed him in arch disbelief, then trilled one of her coquettish laughs. "Well, can't say you look like a couch potato. More like an action man. Which is why you should be buying *Nick's Knickers*. A great turn-on, believe me. Jules tries them out on me to measure response."

"He…models them…for your approval?" Quin asked, pouncing on the chance to draw more information.

"Hey! I don't let him stop at modelling." Jade smooched up to her totally committed partner in every sense. "Do I, honey-bun?" she purred.

"Stokes the fire every time," Jules said with happy satisfaction.

It gave Quin satisfaction, too, having no doubt now that business was mixed with pleasure with this duo, confirming Nicole's availability for his own interest. "Nothing like personal endorsement," he said appreciatively. "Next time I'm shopping for underwear, I'll look for your range."

"No *wife* to choose it for you, Quin?" Nicole slid in coolly, trying to ward off the heat she knew he was going to turn on her.

"No. No wife," he quickly asserted.

"Perhaps I should have said partner," she drawled. "As I recall, you were commitment-shy."

"On the contrary, I'd say I had a history of excessive commitment." He effected an ironic grimace. "Unfortunately, not always choosing the right priority at the right time, much to my regret. I plan on correcting that error in judgment."

"Lucky for the woman you're with now," Nicole rolled back at him, burning over the smooth reference to regrets. Quin was a master at pressing the right buttons to get what he wanted and from the amount of forceful energy being directed at her, she had no doubt he was hunting her head for a new round of pillow-talk in the very near future.

He shrugged. "I'm not *with* any particular woman."

"You mean no one of any importance," she mocked, knowing the only people of importance to Joaquin Sola were those who served his ambition.

"Every person has value," he quickly slung at her, the clever grey eyes giving her a flatteringly high evaluation on the desirability scale.

"You're right," she agreed silkily, her own eyes sizzling with challenge as she added, "but to some people, money counts for a lot more than anyone's value."

Her eyes were locked onto his, watching his sharp intelligence go to work on the conflicts that had ruptured their relationship five years ago.

"Let's not pretend money doesn't count, Nicole. It adds a value to everyone. Like it or not, it's the way the world works," he asserted sardonically.

Too true. And the bottom was going to fall out of her world for the lack of it. A surge of hatred for all the moneymakers who cared for nothing else poured acid into her voice.

"How are you measuring your worth these days, Quin?" she mocked, goaded into striking directly at him. "Have you reached your target yet? How many million were you aiming for? Or was there no fixed number in your mind, just a cumulative amount that could never be enough?"

He cocked his head, weighing the load of bitterness he'd probably heard in her words. "What would you consider enough, Nicole?" he asked softly. "What would meet your needs?"

For a moment she was seduced by the thought that Quin might now have deep enough pockets to actually come to the rescue. But that would involve him in her life, and if she opened one door to him…no, she couldn't go there. Far more would be at stake than the financial ruin she and her mother were facing. Some wreckages one could recover from. Others lasted a lifetime.

She looked at him with arch scepticism and said, "*My* needs were never part of your equation."

"I'd like to make them so."

"Since when? Two minutes ago? The moment you decided to break in on my night out?"

"If the intention is sincere, the timing shouldn't be relevant."

She shook her head at this arrogant belief that her past experience with him and the years between then and now could simply be dismissed. "It's a bit late to be showing interest in me, Quin, and quite frankly, I have none in you," she stated bluntly.

"It shouldn't ever be too late to make some amends on past mistakes," he argued.

"Raking over dead ashes is hardly profitable," she mocked.

"Amazing how often a live ember is found."

He was just as aware as she was that the chemistry between them was still active. It had led her down a destructive path once and Nicole was determined it would not take her there again. "A spark of fool's gold, Quin," she strongly asserted.

"Not if it can be fanned into a flame. It's a cold life without fire, Nicole."

"I'm sure there are many warm hearths that would welcome you."

"One burnt more brightly than any other. I'd like to find my way back to it."

"Unfortunately I can't provide you with a magic door. You'll have to look elsewhere." She waved her hand in conclusive farewell. *Hasta la vista.*

He nodded an acknowledgment of her dismissal, but there was no acceptance of defeat in his eyes as he answered, "Until we meet again." A whimsical little smile was directed at Jade and Jules. "A pleasure to make your acquaintance."

"And fascinating to make yours," Jade instantly replied, goggle-eyed over the encounter.

"Try *Nick's Knickers,*" Jules advised. "Magic door every time."

Quin laughed, saluting them both as he moved off, no doubt warming himself with the satisfaction of knowing he'd made a winning impression on her friends.

Nicole gritted her teeth. One favourable comment about him from either Jade or Jules and she'd explode. The duel of words with Quin had left her pumped up—typical of any exchange between them. He'd got to her. He always had, putting an electric charge under her skin. No other man had ever come close to affecting her as Quin did, but that didn't mean he was good for her. No way! And something savage in her wanted him to taste defeat— taste it, know it, hate it as much as she had.

Both Jade and Jules were looking at her as though they were seeing an entirely different woman to the Nicole they were familiar with, eyes avid with curiosity but mouths firmly buttoned until she opened up. Which she was not about to do. The door was shut on Joaquin Luis Sola.

"There's no going back," she stated flatly. "I don't live at that address anymore."

"The one you shared with him?" Jade quickly speculated.

"It wasn't a place of sharing. It was a place of possession. Always on his terms."

"Bad place," Jules muttered sympathetically.

Nicole nodded. "I live in a different space now."

"Maybe you've made your current space too tight," Jade posed seriously. "What if he no longer lives at that address, either? Time and timing—" she wriggled her fingers "—very tricky things. Shifting sands, different circumstances, revolving doors…how long ago was it when you and Quin were an item?"

Jade had not been in Australia then, but if Nicole pinpointed the time it would be like handing her friend a bone she would gnaw at with intolerable persistence. Jade was far too adept at putting two and two together.

"Doesn't matter," she said, shrugging as she stood up from the table. "Distance has not made the heart grow fonder so just let this one go. Okay? I'm off to the powder room."

"Seems a terrible waste," she heard Jade mutter in a disgruntled tone.

Nicole made good her escape, hoping the subject of Quin would not be revived when she returned. Even so, the fun had gone out of the evening. Just knowing he was here made her feel tense, her nerves prickling with the sense of a dangerous threat to the life she'd made without him.

She wished she could just walk away right now, but leaving the club would signal a vulnerability she didn't want to reveal, not to Jade and Jules, and certainly not to Quin Sola. If he was watching, if he came after her…no, she had to act as though she was totally impervious to his presence.

The powder room provided a safe refuge though she could only take a brief respite there if she was not to give the impression of hiding. The place was crowded—a queue for toilet cubicles and a crush of women along the vanity bench; washing hands, repairing make-up, restoring hairstyles. Nicole joined the queue and tried to block memories of Quin from crawling through her mind by eavesdropping on others' conversations. Ironically, not even here was she free of him.

"So how goes it with Quin Sola?"

The question came loud and clear through the babble of general chat, drawing Nicole's startled gaze to a pretty brunette in red who was looking archly at a tall beautiful blonde, definitely out of the same mould as Paris Hilton, dressed in a second skin blue mini-dress and practising a sexy pout in the mirror.

"Oh, I don't know that he's worth having," she drawled.

"Not worth having! The hottest trader in town? Everyone with any money is using his financial services company. The guy has made billions. And he's an eye-candy hunk, as well."

His company...*billions*...not the star player for an international bank anymore, Nicole realised. Somewhere along the past five years Quin must have moved to being his own man, no doubt accumulating far more personal wealth by working on *his* terms.

"Wow! Point me in his direction," someone eagerly requested, triggering a cheerful chorus of "Me, too," from other chance listeners.

The outburst was ignored.

"I really don't need his money, Nina, and going to bed with a cold fish does not appeal," the blonde said in a bored tone.

The brunette in red grinned. "You mean you made a move on him and he didn't bite."

Mistake, Nicole thought sardonically. Quin made the moves. He was programmed that way. The blonde shrugged as though she didn't care, although her ego had to be suffering some damage. She was wrong about Quin's coldness in bed but his decision-making was icily absolute, no melting around the edges when his mind was made up.

Until we meet again...

A convulsive shiver ran down Nicole's spine as the thought struck her that Quin might have been cold to the blonde because he'd already fixed his sights on herself. What if he didn't accept the rejection she'd just handed out? Five years ago she had fled to Europe to break all connection with him, but she couldn't do that now. She could only hope he would change his mind about pursuing another meeting, leave her alone.

The woman behind her nudged her towards the most recently vacated toilet cubicle. Nicole hadn't even realised she now headed the queue. Nor had she noticed the two women who'd been talking about Quin make their exit from the powder room but they were gone. She hurried forward and closed herself into the small private space, wishing she could close out all the worries whirling around her mind.

From what she'd heard, Quin could easily afford to lend her the money needed to keep the dance school afloat. He might even do it if he got what he wanted from her. If it was only sex…

Nicole shocked herself with the treacherous desire that had prompted that thought. It was so stupid to want Quin for anything. He'd stripped her of self-esteem once. To even dally with an idea that would give him the power to do it again, was just plain crazy.

But she would be using him this time…using him to meet her needs. A vengeful streak in her whispered this was a justifiable course. After all, Quin put a money value on everything. Why shouldn't she?

A controlled situation could be set up—no intrusion on her real life. She wouldn't be hurt by confusing sex with love again. Not with Quin. In fact, there was a lot of savage appeal in turning the tables on him, only giving what she was prepared to give…on *her* terms!

The big question was…how much did Quin want her?

CHAPTER THREE

QUIN's mind and body were firing on all cylinders, energised by the excitement of a challenging chase. He wasn't about to let Nicole escape him this time. However many obstacles she put in his path, he was determined on getting past them, breaking down her resistance and making her his woman again.

What he needed now was some information—where she was working, how her daily schedule ran. It would be easy enough then to set up another *chance* meeting so he could reinforce the mutual attraction she was trying to deny, work on it, build the sparks into a flame that would burn up her opposition to any future together.

He caught sight of Tony watching him make his way back to the party. Quin had learnt in his four years of professional and personal association with him, very little escaped Tony Fisher's notice. Whether it was taking care of legal matters or his keen observation of people, the man was invariably on the ball. He was short and rather stocky, but big with personality, aided by an infectious smile, wickedly merry brown eyes and a wild mop of chestnut curls framing his good-humoured face.

Having sidled around his boisterous guests, he caught Quin just before he joined them. "Trust you to pick out the expert in this crowd," he remarked, nodding in Nicole's direction.

For once, Quin wasn't tuned to Tony's wavelength. "Expert?" he queried.

"The dancing teacher," Tony supplied, raising his eyebrows in arch surprise. "You're slipping if you didn't find that much out about her."

Quin frowned. Tony wasn't making sense. Nicole had been in banking before going overseas. Armed with a top level business degree, she'd worked her way up to the key division of sales, making the most of big investors' money. One of the great things about their relationship had been her understanding of his work on the trading floor.

Though she could certainly dance like a

professional—a natural at Latin American. Even so, Tony must have mistaken her for someone else. A woman with Nicole's brain for clever commerce had to be earning big bucks somewhere in the workplace and that would not be in a school for dancing.

"I think you've got it wrong here, Tony," he mocked his friend who prided himself on getting everything right.

One eyebrow lowered. The other was cocked higher. "Were you or were you not chatting up Nicole Ashton?"

Her name sent a shock wave up Quin's spine. Alert signals shot along his nervous system. He eyed his friend very sharply, seeking urgent entry into his mind. "What do you know about her?"

Tony's mouth formed a curious little smile. "Did she give you the flick?"

Quin tensed as he realised there was definitely some personal previous acquaintance here and he didn't like it. Tony would be unaware of his own past relationship with Nicole. It was before his time, so *the flick* question couldn't relate to that. Which meant it had to come from Tony's own experience with her.

"You have a good reason for asking that?"

he said coldly, hating the thought of his friend having intimate knowledge of Nicole.

"Oh, just that I failed to get anywhere with her beyond the dancing lessons I paid for," he answered with a shrug. "That doesn't happen very often. I might not have the pulling power of your physical assets, but when I set out to charm a woman, I usually win her."

Quin knew that was true, which was why his gut had suddenly been in knots. "But you had no luck with Nicole Ashton," he pressed.

"Not one flirtatious spark from her," came the reassuring reply. "Always pleasant but her focus was fixed on feeling the dance, not feeling anything else. Not with me, anyway."

Relief coursed through Quin. His mind lifted out of a storm of black possessiveness and honed in on getting information. "When was this, Tony?"

"Two years ago. You know me, Quin. I hate not being ahead of the game, and Latin American dancing was becoming popular. I took a month of lessons from her to get all the moves under my belt."

"At a dancing school."

"Yes."

"Evening lessons?" He couldn't believe it was Nicole's day job.

Tony nodded. "Three times a week. Personal tuition, not a class. And all I ever found out about her was she helped run the school for her mother who owned it. Oh, and she'd won a lot of dancing competitions when she was a kid. Had photos and trophies on show to prove it. Like I said…an expert."

She'd never told him this. But then, he'd never told her about his childhood, either. He'd wanted her to accept him as he was at the time—no probing into the past—and having cut off the subject of family several times, insisting that their backgrounds were totally irrelevant to how they felt together, Nicole had given up on trying to change his attitude.

"Where is this school?" he asked, wondering if Nicole had actually gone into business with her mother.

"Burwood."

The suburb was reasonably close to the inner city where he lived and worked but far enough away for their paths to stay apart, given that Burwood was where she lived, as well as worked.

"So you didn't even get that far with her," Tony observed.

"I was just touching base, Tony, feeling for an opening."

"Any crack of encouragement?"

"None. But that was only the initial foray."

"From which you retreated in good order so you could take the fight to her again," Tony dryly deduced.

Quin smiled at his shrewd reading of the situation. "I do not accept that all is lost."

"Well, good luck, my friend. Nicole Ashton looks hot but she's one cool lady."

Not in bed, Quin thought.

"Ah, here's Nina and Amber back from the powder room," Tony announced, looking over Quin's shoulder and holding out an inviting arm for Nina Salter-Smythe—his current love interest—to be gathered in to his side.

Quin swung around to greet the two women's return, surreptitiously using the opportunity to glance back to where Nicole was seated, wanting to catch her looking at him, hoping for another chance to prove that her show of disinterest was not sustainable.

She wasn't there.

His heart thumped with the shock of finding her place vacant.

Had she left the club, intent on doing another runner before he could catch her back?

His gaze jerked to her friends who still

occupied the table. Jade Zilic and her partner, Jules, had their heads together as though plotting something. Surely they would have accompanied Nicole out, at least to see her into a taxi, if she had gone.

Quin told himself it didn't matter, either way.

He had enough information to find her.

CHAPTER FOUR

When Nicole emerged from the powder room, the dance floor was once again crowded, couples throwing themselves into the cha-cha with much energetic panache. This left an easy passage for her back to the table where Jade and Jules remained seated, watching the action.

"Got to say Quin Sola is a superb dancer," Jade immediately commented, pointing to where he was partnering the brunette in red from the powder room. "Did you teach him, Nicole?"

She shook her head. "It's natural to him. He once told me dancing is an expression of life in South America. He grew up with it."

"Where in South America?" Jules asked, his curiosity piqued.

"I don't know. He would never say."

"Ah! A mysterious past," Jade pounced, waggling her highly mobile eyebrows.

"Whatever…" Nicole waved dismissively. "He became an Australian citizen and left the past in the past. Now why don't you two go and dance? I'm happy to sit this one out."

She didn't want to talk about Quin.

She needed more time alone to think about him.

Jade and Jules obligingly left her to it.

Sexual memories bombarded her mind as she watched him dance, his strong, muscular legs snapping out the cha-cha rhythm, his taut cheeky butt almost mesmerising in its matching action. Quin *was* a great dancer. Better than Jules. Best on the dance floor, in fact. Best at everything.

Except actually caring about someone, Nicole savagely reminded herself. The trick with Quin was to take what he offered of himself, enjoy it, and not care back. She simply hadn't been capable of doing that when she'd been with him, caring too much about too many things and losing her own sense of self-worth because he hadn't responded in kind.

She shouldn't have measured herself by that.

The fault lay in Quin, not her.

Five years ago it had been a matter of survival to walk away from him and his lack of caring. Now she was facing a different issue of survival, based on the one commodity Quin apparently had in plenty. Since he put a money value on everything, she wondered how much he would give to warm himself at her hearth. Could she steel herself to shut out *everything else* and put the question to him?

If he said no...well, that was that, nothing lost, nothing gained.

If he said yes...since he'd more or less limited their previous relationship to the bedroom, it seemed logical he'd accept that same limitation again, so there should be no great risk in such an arrangement. In fact, satisfying the desire he was stirring up might do her a power of good. It was Quin who had caused the hole Jade perceived in Nicole's love life. A short, sharp dose of him might cure the long hangover from having been his possession.

Control was the key.

She had to hold it, not let Quin take it over.

Could she do it?

Could she?

The dance ended.

She watched him escort the brunette in red off the dance floor. Jade and Jules were noisily approaching their table. Bold, enterprising Jade. *She* wouldn't think twice about approaching Quin for help if she needed it from him. Striking deals were second nature to her. *Seize the day,* she'd say. *Make it yours.*

Nicole rose to her feet, standing firmly on her stiletto heels, moving forward with determined purpose. "I'm going to speak to Quin Sola," she informed her friends in passing.

Either he caught sight of her approach in some mirrored surface, or his personal antennae picked up her churning chemistry and swung him around to face her, negating any need to break into his social group. She halted a metre away, her mouth tilting into a wry little smile as she tossed at him, "I have a proposition for you, Quin."

He nodded towards the bar. "Let me buy you a drink."

The move would ensure some privacy from his companions, which certainly suited Nicole. It would also prolong this encounter which undoubtedly suited him since she'd cut him off earlier tonight. "Thank you. I'd like that," she replied, her ready agreement bringing a smile of satisfaction to his lips.

He led off without a backward glance at the people he'd been with, instantly making

her the exclusive focus of his attention, shep-
herding her through the crowd without
actually touching her—quite a masterful op-
eration with people in front of them moving
aside at the commanding wave of his hand or
a look into the bullet grey eyes.

The force, Nicole thought. Quin had
always had it—the power to draw or repel
people at will. It was some form of energy
he knew how to exert. Or maybe it was an
innate thing in him, a kind of charisma he'd
been born with. It made him special, out of
the ordinary, and dangerous because it was
all too easy to fall under his spell and then
you belonged to him.

Even knowing this and being on guard
against it, Nicole felt every nerve in her body
quivering with excitement at being close to
the source of this treacherous power.
Locking horns with Quin on any ground was
tantamount to playing with fire. But she had
learnt lessons from being burnt. Nothing
would induce her to let this man take over her
life again. She'd go so far with him and no
further.

They reached the bar and despite the crush
of thirsty people, somehow space was made
for them and a waiter was ready to take their

order. "Two margaritas," Quin told him, not offering Nicole any choice, assuming command of the situation as he always had. But it was not going to be all his way this time, Nicole fiercely determined.

She recalled only too sharply that he'd bought them both margaritas on the very first evening they'd spent together. If he thought he could stir some sentimentality with the memory, he could think again. The cocktails were made. Quin handed over some notes and told the waiter to keep the change. Nicole took her glass, not waiting for it to be handed to her.

Quin picked up his and raised it in a toast. "To second meetings. And second thoughts," he said whimsically, his eyes warmly welcoming her apparent change of mind.

She baulked at entering into any flirtatious banter. Nothing had to be won from Quin. He either went for the deal or he didn't. "You asked me what would meet my needs," she reminded him with sharp directness.

"I did," he agreed, adopting a more attentive expression. "Have you been concocting a list?"

She ignored that question. "You said you'd like to make them your business."

"Within reason," he quickly amended, his eyes more calculating now.

She sipped her margarita, needing to loosen up her taut nerves, hoping a good slug of alcohol would do it. Having worked up the courage to deliver the next line, she plunged on. "You said money adds a value to everyone."

He sipped his drink, silently weighing the thrust of her statements before laying out his interpretation of them. "Are you telling me you have a primary need for money, and if I bring enough to the table, it will open *the magic door?*"

"An urgent need," she corrected him. "So the question is, Quin, how much are you willing to give to get me back into your bed?"

"Give," he repeated, eyes narrowing. "We're not talking about a loan?"

"No." Her chin lifted belligerently, silently defying whatever he was thinking of her. It didn't matter. Only the chance of a positive outcome mattered. "We're talking about an outright gift. And it has to be available to me tomorrow," she spelled out unequivocally.

"And when will you be available to me, Nicole, assuming that I accept your proposition?"

Her heart was pounding at the possibility he would accept. She hadn't really believed it enough to work out how she would manage her side of the deal. What *was* possible for her, given her other commitments? She had to keep him away from her mother's home at Burwood.

"Where do you live now, Quin?"

"I have an apartment at Circular Quay."

Getting public transport to Circular Quay was not a problem—a twenty-minute train trip from Burwood. With a heavy sense of irony, she said, "I could warm the hearth of your home on two nights a week for…" What would be a reasonable offer for the money involved? There had to be a time limit.

"For as long as I want you," he pushed.

"No!" That would be handing control to him. "For three months," she quickly decided, not caring what he thought of it, intuitively knowing she couldn't risk more. Three months was as fair a bargain as she was prepared to offer.

"Twenty-six nights…" he said musingly, his eyes smoking with memories of sexual highs with her.

Panic galloped through Nicole. She hadn't

done the maths, just grabbed at a time limit. Could she sustain objectivity with Quin for that long, hold the line she had to hold?

It was impossible to recant now. Quin would instantly pick up on how vulnerable she felt about it. Besides, he himself might baulk when it came to the cost of those twenty-six nights with her. No doubt he could get a high class callgirl to satisfy his every desire for much less.

"How much money do you need, Nicole?" he asked, coming straight to the point.

Her own eyes issued a mocking challenge as she replied with the total figure of the debts to be paid. "Seven hundred and thirty-six thousand dollars and fifty-five cents." The numbers were deeply imprinted on her mind from having been so terribly plagued by them.

Quin digested them without so much as a flicker of an eyelid, maintaining a poker face as he checked on what she'd said before. "And you need it tomorrow."

"Yes."

"Or what will happen?"

She shook her head. "That's private. This is a take it or leave it proposition. You say yes or no."

"Spend tonight with me while I consider it."

"No! I'm not giving out freebies, Quin. I won't spend a night with you until you give me my value in money and it has to be given tomorrow."

"Your value…" he drawled derisively.

"You used those words," she fiercely reminded him, her stomach churning with the anticipation of imminent humiliation. "Yes or no," she repeated.

His eyes glittered with plans of his own as he reached out and took her glass from her, a glass that was empty although she couldn't recall having drunk all its contents. She saw that his was empty, too, as he placed both glasses on the bar. So this mad encounter was at an end, she thought, steeling herself to turn her back on it.

"I'll give you my answer after you dance this tango with me," he said with a relish that sent warning tingles down her spine.

Nicole was given no time to respond, no time to resist. Her hand was captured by his and strongly held as he pulled her after him, onto the dance floor. The band had only just started up again. No other couples had begun dancing. Quin swung her into the centre of the empty floor, then lifted her arms, arrogantly positioning the initial embrace for the traditional start of the tango.

Her body arched back in instinctive resistance as he assumed the dominant role, his strong legs forcing hers into the *salida,* the basic walking pattern, which Quin turned into a physical—*sexual*—stalking, igniting a volatile energy in Nicole that sizzled with the need to challenge him, fight him, beat him at his own game.

It was more than a matter of pride to match his perfectly executed figure-eights, his turns, twists and sweeps. Every chance she had she threw in some fancy embellishments to the hooks and kicks, challenging him to meet her creativity, beat it if he could. It goaded him to hurl her into a masterful drag, making her submit to a feet together slide, then swiftly engineering a *sandwich,* trapping her thigh against his, leaning into her, his arm circling her waist in possessive support as she arched back, his hand almost cupping the soft swell of her breast.

"Don't think you can take, Quin," she shot at him.

"Just checking the merchandise," he retorted.

Nicole's blood boiled at the crass term but there was no point in taking offence since it was in keeping with her proposition. Besides, it was best she knew Quin thought of her like that—a strong deterrent to any emotional attachment forming.

Merchandise…

She'd show him merchandise!

The intricate footwork and dark passion of their tango had drawn spectators who stood back, clapping them on, leaving them plenty of room to indulge themselves in the dramatic rhythm of the music. Nicole recklessly abandoned herself to the sexuality of the dance with a wild display of provocative wiggles and shakes until Quin claimed her again, sweeping her into a whirl of double-time steps, then re-establishing his dominance with a high lift and a body curl around him. Nicole hit back with a full contact downward slide which gave her undeniable evidence of his excitement.

"Nothing without the money, Quin," she reminded him, exulting in the hard bulge of his erection.

His eyes blazed raw desire at her. "Don't tell me you're not on fire, Nicole."

"You won't break my resolve," she taunted

and maintained a haughty disdain through-out his heat-seeking manoeuvres for the rest of the dance.

They were breathing hard when the music ended, her breasts heaving against his chest, their bodies bent in the traditional aggressive/resistant pose, her head, shoulders and arms straining away from him, her long hair almost sweeping the floor, his face hovering over hers. Although loud applause broke out around them, neither of them acknowledged it. Quin wasn't yet ready to break from the sizzling sexuality of this last embrace.

"Admit you want me!" he demanded.

"Prove that you value what I can give you," she counter-demanded.

"Tomorrow morning, the money. Tomorrow night, you come to me."

"Agreed."

His eyes glittered with animal savagery. "I'll have my pound of flesh, Nicole."

But not my heart, she thought with the same depth of ferocity. Quin Sola couldn't take it twice.

"Twenty-six nights," he reaffirmed.

"Payment in full," she promised.

"I'll hold you to it."

"I know."

"As long as you understand there is no escape clause."

"Understood."

"Right! So let's get down to necessary details."

He scooped her upright again and released her from his embrace, retaining only her hand as he swung her out beside him to perform an acknowledging bow to the still applauding spectators. Their faces were a blur to Nicole. She was gripped by a weird sense of shock that the deal had actually been made. Quin was going to pay off the ruinous debt and she was about to become his sex slave for three months.

Being his sex slave was not something new, she sternly told herself, just a repetition of the past, but her legs started wobbling as they made their way back to the bar. Neither she nor Quin were inclined to head for their respective tables since there was still private business to be done. She hoped he understood that their negotiated intimacy should remain private, too.

"Another drink?" Quin asked.

"Just iced water," she replied.

He ordered two, probably feeling the same need to cool down. While they waited, a man came up and clapped Quin on the shoulder, claiming his attention and making Nicole's nerves even more jumpy.

"Got to say you've met your match, Quin," he rolled out with a grin, twinkling brown eyes spreading his good humour to both of them. "Great dancing! You should snag him for a partner if you're still doing dance competitions, Nicole."

Shock hit her hard, squeezing her heart and making her stomach contract in fear.

Tony Fisher!

She remembered giving him dancing lessons—something like two years ago—but she couldn't remember how she'd been working her situation at the time. Did he know about Zoe? Would he mention her to Quin? How closely were the two men connected?

"Tony…" she greeted him belatedly.

"Glad you remember me." He exuded happy warmth as he offered his hand.

She took it briefly. "Not many men have so much charm. I hope you're enjoying your own dancing."

"I am, indeed. As to charm…" He flicked a wry smile at Quin. "It seems my friend has considerably more."

Friend!

"Not so I've noticed," she said coolly. "But then, charm isn't a necessary component when doing business. The primary aim is to understand each other. Quin and I are trying to settle the details of an agreement, so if you'd be so kind as to…"

"Leave you alone together? Got it!" He raised a hand in a salute to both of them and moved away.

Quin handed her a long glass of iced water. "Very deft," he commented. "A pity you're wasting your talent for handling people in a dance school."

So he knew that much. "Believe me, it's not wasted there," she said dryly. When he made no other observation about her current life, Nicole's tension eased a little. "Let's tie this up quickly before we're interrupted again," she said briskly. "Are you carrying a business card with your e-mail address on it?"

"Yes." He put his drink down to get the card out of his wallet and give it to her. "Do you have yours in your handbag?"

"You won't need it. I'll e-mail you when I get home tonight, spelling out where the money has to be transferred. You can reply to sender, giving me your home address and what time you want me to arrive."

"That works," he agreed.

Nicole wanted to get away from him now, escape the tension of being this close. She had to spend twenty-six nights in his company but tonight wasn't one of them. "I want this deal kept private, Quin," she quickly stated.

His eyes mocked her concern. "I'm hardly likely to spread the fact that I have to buy sex from you."

A tide of scorching heat rushed up her neck and burnt her cheeks. "You didn't value it when I *gave* it to you," she fired back at him.

"I'll count the worth of every second this time."

"Do that!" Her chin lifted in defiant denial of any more seconds on the clock with him now. "In the meantime, please excuse me. My friends are probably wondering where I am."

"Oh, I don't think they're wondering, Nicole. Not after our tango. But I'll escort you back to their table to ensure they know you've been in good hands."

"I don't need to be escorted, thank you," she flashed at him as she turned to go.

"I wouldn't want your friends to think I'm not gentleman enough to give you that courtesy," came the insidiously determined voice behind her.

Nicole gritted her teeth and said no more, knowing there'd be no shaking him off until he performed his self-appointed role. Waste of breath to argue. In actual fact, Quin had always played the gentleman with women; opening doors, seeing them seated, extending protection whenever it was appropriate. It had once given Nicole the sense of being cherished, but his courtesies had nothing to do with cherishing. Quin simply followed standards he'd set for himself.

She sailed ahead, acutely aware of him trailing closely in her wake and inwardly stewing over how she was going to explain what she'd been doing with Quin to Jade and Jules. No doubt they had seen the tango performance, which certainly didn't gel with banishing the man from her life. There had been nothing cold about it, either.

Quin had caught up and was shoulder to shoulder with her when they arrived at the table. Both Jade and Jules had wide grins on their faces, probably thinking they'd been witnessing the rebirth of a passionate affair.

Before Nicole could issue a polite dismissal to Quin, Jade surprised her by holding out a brilliant yellow butterfly, exquisitely fashioned from silk with silver glitter outlining its wings.

"For your tree," she rushed out. "I made it to brighten you up. Not that you probably need it now but I thought I'd give it to you before the two of you make off out of the club." Her eyes sparkled delight. "It can mark this reunion with Quin."

"It's beautiful, Jade. Thank you. But…"

"What tree?" Quin cut in before Nicole could deny the double departure Jade was obviously anticipating.

"The butterfly tree," Jules supplied. "It's a great fantasy décor piece. The branches are made of driftwood and…"

Nicole panicked, afraid he was about to mention Zoe. "It's a private thing, Jules," she warned, her eyes stabbing the point home. "And you're mistaken, Jade. Quin and I are not going off together. We were simply settling an old score between us." She quickly turned to Quin and held out her hand. "Thank you. We do have everything settled, don't we?"

He gripped hard, his eyes probing hers with nerve-tearing intensity. "Time will tell," he said, the sense of threat behind his words warning Nicole she had better deliver her side of the deal.

She nodded. "I won't keep you from your party any longer."

His mouth curled into a sardonic little smile. "Nor I from yours."

To her intense relief he said good night to Jade and Jules, taking his leave without another word. Which left her with the task of fending off their curiosity for the rest of the evening at the club. Fortunately they didn't want to stay late as they had an important business meeting in the morning. By one o'clock Nicole had been driven home and she was seated at her computer, ready to transmit the necessary figures for Quin to rescue her mother from losing everything.

Her fingers hesitated over the keyboard.

She stared at the e-mail address on the card he'd given her.

This was the point of no return.

Total bankruptcy or twenty-six nights with Quin.

Her chest felt very tight.

Don't think about it, she fiercely told herself. Just do it.

CHAPTER FIVE

NICOLE tried to relax as the train carried her into the city centre for her rendezvous with Quin. The day had been loaded with stress— many phone-calls checking if the money had come through, confirming that all debts had been paid on time. Also, it had been impossible to avoid telling her mother how *the miracle* had come about since the two nights out a week had to be explained, especially since tonight was the first one. She needed her mother to look after Zoe.

The relief of having been saved from bankruptcy had quickly disintegrated into hand-wringing guilt over the deal Nicole had made with Quin Sola. "You would never have gone back to him but for me," her mother had wailed.

"It's only three months, Mum," Nicole had argued. "It won't kill me. In fact, it's much more acceptable than having to lose this home and the dancing school."

Which would have totally devastated her mother.

Nicole knew that her own qualifications, persistence and presentation would have eventually won a job somewhere in the finance world—a job with a big enough salary to support them. This would not have been *the end* for her. But these losses, on top of the loss of her beloved second husband, would have tipped her mother into a deeper depression, possibly paralysing her will to do anything. Perhaps now, some sense of responsibility for getting into this mess might pull her into plotting some positive course for her future with the dancing school.

The train arrived at Circular Quay and Nicole promptly disembarked. Quin's e-mail had instructed her to meet him at a restaurant called Pier Twenty-One, situated on Benelong Point near the Opera House. She glanced at her watch as she started the walk past the ferry terminal. It was a few minutes short of eight o'clock, the nominated time.

She walked fast, not wanting to be late. Quin had kept his word. Keeping hers was essential. It was not only a matter of integrity, but pride, as well. She would not give Quin any cause to criticise her over the delivery of her side of the deal. He had paid out a phenomenal amount of money for his twenty-six nights.

Nevertheless, she had baulked at dressing up as though for a dinner date. There was no romance in this arrangement and she didn't want Quin to think there could be in her mind. If he chose to spend his time with her eating in a restaurant—fine!—she would eat with him. No doubt they would eventually end up in bed together, which was what tonight was really about.

She'd decided to wear jeans, flat walking sandals and one of the filmy floral tops that were currently fashionable for teaming with jeans—day or night. She would wear the same things when she left him tomorrow morning. Her small overnight bag only held some toiletry articles and a change of under-wear. As long as her mind was set on con-ducting this specifically limited affair on a completely practical basis, she should not get into an emotional tangle over it.

Quin's table had a front row view of the pass-ing parade of people; commuters catching a ferry home, tourists taking in the sights of arguably the most spectacular harbour in the world, theatre-goers heading for their choice of entertainment; concert, ballet, play, opera. The outdoors dining section of the restaurant extended out beyond the great marble colonnade that sheltered the many boutiques, bars and restaurants along the way to the huge Opera House forecourt. It was a fine summer evening, a fantastic setting, but Quin's entire focus was fixed on watching for Nicole.

He had no doubt she would turn up at the appointed time and place, probably arriving at the quay early to ensure punctuality, and loitering somewhere nearby so as not to give him more of herself than she had to. Quin had no illusions about what had driven her to this deal—extreme duress over a financial situation, linked to a highly personal sense of payback for how he had conducted their previous relationship. It was the latter motivation that exercised his mind now. The money side of it was done.

He wanted sex with her and he would certainly have it, but his prime directive tonight was to challenge where she was coming from, sabotage her game-plan, make her play to his rules. She'd put a fire in his belly last night. The fight was on to get everything he wanted from Nicole Ashton and with twenty-six nights up his sleeve, Quin was confident of carrying out a siege that would eventually smash her defences and make her surrender all she was to him.

He'd had that once from her.

He wanted it again, free of the demons that had driven much of his life.

There she was!

Nothing hesitant about her approach.

She was striding out, unhampered by any tight sexy skirt or high heels. Her long legs were clad in blue denim and the flat sandals on her feet signalled casual comfort had priority over any female urge to excite desire in him. Clearly she didn't care what he thought or felt. It was unimportant to her. Her head was bent in private thought, a look of determined purpose on her face. She wasn't looking for him. She was simply making her way to the meeting place.

He noted the overnight bag she was carrying—only big enough to hold a few essentials—definitely no frills on Nicole's agenda tonight. Her long curly hair was loose, no tantalising pins to remove. The top she wore was more feminine than the unisex jeans, but not a *look at me* garment. Quin smiled to himself. If she thought her presentation would put him off the merchandise, she could think again.

As though she suddenly sensed his scrutiny, her head lifted, gaze swinging sharply towards where he sat, connecting with his, flashing a wry acknowledgment of *game on*. Her feet halted as she watched him rise from the table, ready to greet her. Quin felt his body zinging with anticipation. A strong blast of intuition told him she was eyeing the enemy before engaging with him. Retreat was not in the air. Let the battle begin, Quin thought, holding out an open hand to draw her in.

Nicole ignored the accelerated pounding of her heart and put on a determinedly cheerful face as she walked forward to greet the man who'd paid the price she'd put on herself. Since he would now expect value for it, an initial smile seemed the best way to get proceedings onto reasonably pleasant terms.

"Quin…" She took his hand, giving it a light squeeze. "Thank you for making the money available so quickly. It made today much less difficult than it could have been."

Just as well she had prepared that little

speech because Quin's strong magnetism was zapping all the sensible thoughts out of her mind. The mere touch of his hand was shooting electric tingles up her arm. She'd put half a world between them to get away from the sexual hold he'd once had on her. Distance had not diminished the power of his attraction but she simply couldn't afford to fall victim to it this time. Somehow she had to keep whatever happened between them contained.

"I've built my business on being efficient and effective," he replied.

"Not to mention ruthless," she slung at him, the words tripping off her tongue, regardless of her earlier resolve not to revive old emotional wounds. Even worse, she withdrew her hand so quickly, her fingernails scraped along his.

His grey eyes glittered with sardonic amusement. "I wondered how long it would take for the claws to come out."

"Sorry. I probably need a manicure."

"I was referring to your description of me."

Ruthless?

"Oh, come now," she chided. "You can't deny one of your greatest attributes—setting a goal and going after it with single-minded dedication."

"I'll concede that attitude has served me well, for the most part."

"Got the results you wanted," she pushed derisively.

"More often than not. I've even got you, Nicole. Which just goes to prove that a huge loss can be recovered—" he grinned provocatively as he added "—if one is ruthless enough."

She raised a mocking eyebrow. "Or prepared to sacrifice a great deal of money."

"But it's not a sacrifice. It's an investment in the future."

"A very short-term future."

"We'll see." He gestured to the chair opposite his at the table. "Please join me. I've ordered champagne to celebrate the beginning of a new chapter in our lives."

Not so new, she thought caustically, curbing her tongue as she settled on the chair. The adrenaline rush of crossing swords with Quin needed to be curbed, as well. It drew her into revealing how much he could still get under her skin and she didn't want to give him that satisfaction.

He signalled to a waiter to open the bottle

of champagne which was sitting in an ice-bucket, conveniently placed on a portable stand beside their table. The waiter handed them menus and reeled off a list of chef's specials as he uncorked the bottle and filled their glasses.

"We'll both have a dozen oysters followed by the lobster in butter sauce with a side salad," Quin said, abrogating any choice Nicole might have made.

She didn't bother protesting, though once the waiter had left she dryly commented, "I might have wanted something else."

"You've got what you wanted, Nicole." He lifted his glass in a toast. "Here's to what I want."

She fiddled with her glass, watching him sip the champagne, his eyes challenging her to make some issue on how he was handling the situation. He knew she loved seafood and had invariably ordered it whenever they had dined out in the past. Lobster was terribly expensive, so in fact he was giving her treat. And knew it. But he was also claiming absolute dominance during her time with him.

"If you want your pound of flesh, Quin, why have me meet you in such a public place?" She gestured to the milling crowd of passers-by.

"They say the flesh is sweeter closer to the bone. I don't mind taking my time working down to it."

Peeling off layer and layer of protective skin, Nicole thought, a convulsive little shiver running down her spine. She couldn't let Quin get too close to her. He might tear her apart if she didn't remain on guard.

"Why not relax?" he invited with a teasing smile. "Obviously you are completely safe here amongst so many people. The night is young and I'm perfectly happy to revel in the exquisite pleasure of anticipation."

"Right!" She lifted her glass, determined on blocking out the more intimate future for a while. "Here's to fine food…"

"Fine company," Quin slid in.

"And fine wine," she finished pointedly, sipping the champagne which was, indeed, very fine.

Nevertheless, it was impossible to relax with Quin sitting opposite her, watching her, silently revelling in his plans for tonight. Get his mind off them, she told herself. Ask him questions. Persist until he did talk about himself. He might even give her answers this time around.

"So how is the banking world these days?" she started.

He shrugged. "I run my own finance company now."

"Trading profitably?"

"That's what I do."

"Tell me about it," she invited.

"The money business is no different to when you were working in a bank, Nicole."

"But the transition from being employed to—"

"The work is the same," he cut her off. "I'd find it far more interesting to hear why you've chosen to teach dancing."

"You haven't changed a bit, have you?" she flared at him.

His eyes glittered with challenging speculation. "What do you want to change about me?"

Nicole quickly retreated from any personal element. "I'm not interested in changing you, Quin," she stated flatly. "I was merely commenting."

"On what?"

She shrugged. "You don't open up about yourself." Suddenly seeing a line of attack, she added, "It makes me wonder what you're afraid of revealing."

"Fear doesn't enter into it," he answered.

"What does then?"

The waiter arrived with their first course. Nicole stared down at the oysters as he refilled their glasses before leaving the two of them alone again.

"This is just what you're like," she shot at Quin. "An oyster with an impenetrable shell."

"I'll let you eat me tonight," he said wickedly.

Sex! That's all it had ever been with Quin. He'd probably ordered the oysters because they were supposed to be an aphrodisiac. She picked up her fork and ate them, her mind skating around memories of Quin's body—his sexually aroused naked body—and how wildly they'd made love in the past. Except it hadn't been making love. It was just sex! Which was what she had to remember at all times with him.

"So why are you working at a dance school, Nicole?" he asked when the plates had been cleared away.

She looked directly into his penetrating grey eyes and defiantly answered, "Private reasons."

His mouth took on an ironic twist. "You know, money always leaves a trail. Mortgage on the school, mortgage on a house, big debt to a money-lender—all attached to one name, and that name is not yours. Who is Linda Ellis?"

The question tapped into a bank of resentment that had never been resolved. "You'd know if you'd ever accepted one of my invitations to meet my mother."

He ignored her reference to the old bone of contention between them. "Your mother. Why the different name?"

"A second marriage."

"Does she have a gambling problem?"

"No. What happened will not happen again."

"How can you be sure of that?"

"Because my stepfather is dead."

Her bald statement gave him pause for thought, a deep frown drawing his black eyebrows together. "*He* bled her of all that money?" he finally asked.

"No. The people who held out false hope bled her of all that money."

She heard the angry frustration in her voice, saw the sharp questions in his eyes and knew she might as well explain how the debts had mounted up, stop any further unwelcome speculation on the subject.

"Harry had liver cancer. My mother spent the last two years of his life taking him around the world to quacks and clinics that promised cures. She wouldn't give up. If there was any chance, any way—" Nicole sighed and gestured her own helplessness over the situation. "It didn't matter what it cost, she kept getting the money to do it. Harry was not going to die because they didn't have the money to save him."

"Blind faith," Quin muttered.

"She loved him," Nicole said defensively, ashamed of her own exasperation with her mother's belief in people who'd preyed on her desperation. It had been hard losing her father when she was fifteen, no doubt even harder for her mother. The thought of losing Harry, too, had probably been unbearable.

"The price of love," Quin mused with a quirky little smile. "The same price I've just paid for you, Nicole. Maybe I should have negotiated for two years instead of taking only three months."

"Not at all. You've got prime time," she retorted mockingly. "Lust burns out much faster than love."

He laughed, adding a megawatt attraction to his handsome face. A warm flood of pleasure swept through Nicole, forcing her to acknowledge that no man before or since Quin Sola had done this to her, arousing such strong feelings she had to ride through them because there was no blocking them.

He leaned towards her, forearms on the table, his eyes dancing with a wicked inner joy. "I have missed you, Nicole," he purred. "Missed you very much."

"Not enough to drop everything and chase after me when I left you," she flipped at him as she leaned away, pressing against the back-rest of her chair, needing to put some steel in her spine, bringing out memories of the past to shield her from the weakening effect of his personal charisma.

His shoulders straightened, the twinkle in his eyes sharpening to a hard glitter. "Proving your power over me? I didn't have time for such games."

"You didn't have time for me."

"Not as much as you wanted, no," he retorted, his voice gathering a harsh intensity. "But more than I've given any other woman, before or since."

"Am I supposed to feel flattered by that?"

"Just stating a fact."

Nicole's cheeks were burning from the hot rush of aggression he'd stirred. She bit her lips, fiercely telling herself to retreat to a neutral place. This kind of exchange was not going to serve any good purpose. Though despite her attempt to regain a calmer composure, her hackles rose again when Quin smiled with wolfish satisfaction.

"You know what is worth every cent of my investment, Nicole?"

She shrugged, pretending disinterest.

"You're honour bound to stay with me— like it or not—for twenty-six nights. No running away from what we are together."

"What are we, Quin?" she asked with arch carelessness.

"I intend for us to be unstoppable."

"And I intend for us to be finally finished."

He grinned, not the least bit turned off by her claim.

He was still grinning as the waiter arrived, served their lobsters and refilled their glasses.

Quin lifted his champagne and said with a lilt of elation, "To a fine start and an even finer finish."

Nicole held her tongue.

But she did lift her glass derisively and drank to his toast. It meant nothing, she told herself. She wouldn't let it. The one thing she was certain about—Quin couldn't be trusted to commit himself to anything other than making money.

CHAPTER SIX

Now to the business end of the evening, Nicole thought, as they left the restaurant. The skin-prickling awareness of Quin walking beside her and the treacherous excitement he generated, made it extremely difficult to keep a level head and an objective attitude about what was going to happen when they reached his apartment.

"It's only a short stroll," he said amiably, showing no tension whatsoever over being with her.

Why would he?

He was in the box seat, directing the action.

It was okay to want sex with him, Nicole told herself. Take it, enjoy it, then leave it behind you when you go in the morning. Just don't believe it's anything else but physical chemistry driving a perfectly natural urge.

After five long celibate years she was enti-tled—as a woman—to feel sexual pleasure again. Probably her highly personal knowl-edge of how Quin had given it in the past was stirring the desire.

"Look!" His hand curled around her arm to hold her still as he pointed to the shop window they were passing.

"At what?"

Her gaze swept around a display of Aus-tralian souvenirs. Being situated here, un-derneath the marble colonnade, the place was very much an upmarket boutique for tourists. A small group of Japanese were inside, stocking up on gifts to take home with them. There were many such shops around Circular Quay, catering for the same trade. This was an expensive one but beyond that...

"The blue butterfly," Quin enlightened her. "Come on. Let's go in and buy it for your tree."

Nicole's heart lurched—the shock of his knowledge only dissipating when she remem-bered he'd queried Jade's gift to her last night. Jules had explained it although she'd stopped him from saying too much. The butterfly tree was a special thing between her and Zoe.

A fierce wave of protest burst through her mind. She didn't want Quin associated with it in any way whatsoever. He didn't have the right to intrude upon it. He hadn't been part of it, never would be part of it. Yet before she could find suitable words to check his impulsive suggestion, his arm was around her waist, scooping her inside the boutique, and as always with Quin, a saleswoman instantly zeroed in on him.

"We want the blue butterfly," he said unequivocally.

"Ah yes, a beautiful piece." The woman smiled at him, then quickly moved to get it out of a glass showcase which contained a menagerie of Australian birds, fish and animals, some exquisitely fashioned in crystal, others delicately made of blown glass with colour swirling through them.

"It's a Ulysses, native to far north Queensland," the saleswoman prattled on. "You see them everywhere up around Cairns and the Daintree Rainforest. The natural colour of their wings is an iridescent electric blue, so you'll get the best effect if you can place this piece where sunlight shines through the delicate glass."

"We'll take it. Wrap it up," Quin instructed.

"Wait!" Nicole cried, frantically trying to come up with a reason to stop this purchase. "It looks terribly expensive. How much is it?"

The price stated was exorbitant. There was probably a huge mark-up on everything in the boutique because of its prime position near the Opera House.

"I can't accept this, Quin," she said firmly.

He looked incredulously at her. "After all you've accepted from me today?" He shook his head, took out his wallet, extracted a credit card and smiled at the saleswoman as he passed it to her. "Wrap it up. It's a perfect memento for a momentous evening."

There was no stopping him from making the purchase. Nicole recognised that. However, she could and would refuse to take the butterfly from him. She kept her arms rigidly at her sides when he tried to hand the boutique bag to her as they left the shop. "This isn't part of our deal," she insisted.

"I bet you haven't got one like it," he pressed temptingly.

"That's not the point."

"What is?"

She flashed a fiercely determined look at him. "I don't want a memento of tonight."

A ruthless gleam answered her. "I intend that you find it unforgettable anyway, Nicole."

Her hands clenched in a blind need to fight off the sense of very real danger to the life she'd made without him. "This will pass," she muttered in savage resolve.

"It didn't last time. Which is why we are here now." His eyes challenged her to deny it.

She couldn't. No-one else would have drawn her into bartering herself for money. It was because of who he was, what he was, and how unimportant he'd made her feel in the past when his obsession about amassing money had come ahead of everything else. But she was not about to admit that Quin was right. Feeding his ego was not on her agenda.

"We're here now because you represented a way out of a situation I didn't want," she stated flatly.

"Which, in turn, represented a way into a situation I did want," he slid back at her. "And both *wants* have their roots in the past... which definitely has not passed, Nicole."

Not for him. It had only been sex on his mind then and he had the hots for her again now. This was just a second round of the same. But it was different for her. She'd been wildly, blindly, heart-wrenchingly in love with him. That definitely had passed.

Not wanting this subject pursued, Nicole kept her mouth firmly shut. Quin waved her to turn under an archway which led into a lobby housing a massive spiral staircase and a bank of elevators—marble tiles on the floor, marble walls, huge chandelier hanging from a ceiling, two storeys high—the kind of place that screamed *exclusive to the very wealthy*.

"Here we are," he announced, using a key to operate one of the elevators.

The doors opened.

Quin ushered her into the softly carpeted compartment, stepped in after her, pressed a button marked P and closed out the rest of the world. P for penthouse, Nicole thought, panic skittering through her stomach as the elevator zoomed up to the private apartment where she would become Quin's penthouse playmate. Would it be more pain than pleasure? Had she been completely mad to enter into this contract?

Think of what had been achieved for her mother, she told herself, trying desperately to appear calm and composed as Quin guided her into a fabulous living room. Dominating it were floor to ceiling windows, giving a spectacular view of Sydney Harbour stretching from Bennelong Point right out to sea. Nicole automatically walked over to it, needing to face something other than Quin's material acquisitions, which had clearly meant more to him than she ever had.

The carpet underfoot was a soft teal colour. There were cream leather couches with lots of colourful scatter cushions, glass tables with creamy granite pedestals holding them up. Just props, Nicole thought in bitter dismissal. Status symbols. Expensive interior decoration did not make a home. Quin had never been interested in making a home.

It was a high view of the harbour. Although it was now dark outside, the foreshore with all its little coves was outlined by the lights of the houses crowding it. Boats riding at anchor could easily be seen, ferries carving through the water to their destinations. Nicole wondered if living up here made Quin feel he was on top of this city, king of his castle.

Did he know how empty his castle was,

despite all his possessions, of which she was now one—but only a very temporary one.

Did he ever think this wasn't enough?

She shook her head over the foolish questions.

They sprang from her own emotions, not his, and she was not—*not*—going to get emotionally involved with Quin Sola again!

Quin stood by the broad serving bench of the open plan kitchen, watching Nicole take in the multimillion dollar view. He made no move to join her, though he sensed she was armour-plating herself against the inevitable intimacy of the bedroom. Her shoulders were rigidly squared. Her stillness seemed to form a self-protective cloak. She would give what she had to give but nothing more.

Under normal circumstances, women coming here for the first time showed some curiosity or interest in his personal living quarters; checking out the furnishings, fossicking through his kitchen, making admiring comments. Nicole's stiff back shut it all out and her silence affirmed her lack of caring. She no more wanted to be part of his life than she wanted him to be part of hers. The adamant rebuff of the butterfly gift underlined her determination to stay detached where it really counted—in her mind and heart.

He felt his own jaw tighten with determination as he looked down at the chic boutique bag he was still carrying. Nicole had used the tissue-wrapped blue butterfly nestled inside as a weapon against him, telling him very sharply he didn't belong in her world and she would not let him put even one small step into it. Nevertheless, her strongly negative reaction to the gift told him he could use it as a weapon, too, hitting at what obviously had some personal meaning to her.

"Would you like some coffee, Nicole?"

"Yes, please," she answered without turning her head.

"You used to like cappuccino. My coffee machine can make it if that's still your preference."

"Yes. Thank you."

A tight flat voice and still no glance around.

It increased Quin's determination to crack the wall she was putting up between them. He made her coffee, opened a small box of Belgium chocolates, set both of them down on the low table which serviced the sofa closest to where she was standing. At the slight clatter of china on the glass surface of the table—or maybe it was the strong scent of the steaming hot coffee—she did turn, finally acknowledging his efforts to please her with a dry little smile.

"Chocolates, too," she said as though mocking any attempt to sweeten her up.

"Since you're so entranced with the view," he drawled, mocking her right back. "I'll leave you to enjoy it while I slip into something more comfortable. Excuse me, won't you?"

The startled look on her face gave him immense satisfaction. He grinned to himself as he headed down the hall to his bedroom. It wasn't *his* comfort on his mind. The aim was to keep tipping Nicole out of any comfort zone she thought she had, and there was nothing more effective to gain ground than a surprise attack.

Nicole frowned in confusion as Quin disappeared down a hall.

Slip into something more comfortable?

That was a woman's line—a woman intent on seducing a man.

What was Quin playing at?

Champagne, oysters, an expensive gift, chocolates…were these things meant to melt some expected resistance to him? It made no sense. He didn't have to play a seductive game to get her into bed. She was his for the taking. That was the deal and she wasn't about to welsh on it.

He was probably getting his gear off to save the inconvenience of undressing later on. Quin had always been perfectly comfortable in his skin. And why not? He had a flawless male physique. Her stomach fluttered at the thought of seeing him naked again.

She moved to the sofa and sat down, sipping the hot creamy cappuccino in the hope of calming her nerves. She didn't touch the chocolates. Taking any of them might suggest she was enjoying herself, thereby giving Quin the satisfaction of thinking he *was* seducing her.

This was not a love affair.

She wouldn't let Quin draw her into thinking it could be.

He was playing a game with her. She couldn't imagine him ever having paid money for sex before. No doubt he wanted to turn it into a conquest so his male ego would triumph over the means to the end he desired.

The coffee cup was empty and still he had not returned to the living room. Was he deliberately holding her in waiting, demonstrating who was now master of this situation?

Stop thinking of him, Nicole silently screamed at herself. He was winning by dominating her thoughts!

She rose from the sofa and returned to gazing at the view. Let him find her where he'd left her, ignoring the penthouse proof of his success at making money. Determinedly blanking her mind to everything else, she stood by the window, staring out.

But her instincts picked up Quin's presence the moment he re-entered the living room. There was no sound of footsteps. He didn't speak. She felt the atmosphere change as though some elemental force made it vibrate with a sudden flow of dynamic energy. She knew he was there, watching her, willing her to turn around and acknowledge him. Her whole body felt the tug of his silent command and she had to steel herself to deny it.

Let him come to her. She was here in his

apartment for the night. That was the letter of the agreement between them. What he wanted to make of it was up to him.

He came. Her heart drummed his approach as though it sensed every footstep bringing him closer and closer to her. Then his hands were on her hips, sliding up underneath her top, unclipping her bra, reaching around to push the lace cups from her breasts, freeing them for his touch, his fingers lightly kneading the soft fullness, his thumbs fanning her nipples to a responsive tautness.

Nicole found herself holding her breath, her whole being consumed with the desire to feel. It had been so long…so very long…and Quin knew how to touch, how to excite, how to build a pool of pleasure that turned her insides to warm liquid. She finally released her breath and quickly sucked in more air as he lifted her top up over her head, removing the bra with it.

"Stay still," he commanded, his fingers raking through her hair, parting it, lifting the long tresses from her back and pushing them over either shoulder to flow down over her breasts.

She stayed still, but could not prevent a

convulsive little shiver as he kissed the bared nape of her neck, his mouth hot and seductively sensual. His fingertips feathered down the curve of her spine, drew tantalising circles on her rib-cage, moved slowly upwards until they reached the fall of her hair which he gently rubbed over her sensitised breasts.

"I always did love the feel of you, Nicole," he murmured.

Don't use the word, *love,* to me, she thought fiercely. Arouse me sexually all you like, but love is something you know nothing about.

His hands glided down to the waistband of her jeans. He pulled the stud apart, opened the zipper. Her stomach contracted under the warmth of his palms spreading over it as his fingers targeted the heat he'd already generated between her thighs. He knew how to touch there, too, softly, softly caressing the folds apart, using her own moistness to tease her clitoris, building an excitement that she knew would drive her beyond all control.

Her breathing quickened, little gasps escaping her lips even as she mentally fought to remain still as though nothing was really happening. She wanted Quin to think her body was simply responding naturally to nothing but expert stimulation. He, as a person, didn't count. She stared unseeingly into the darkness of the night sky, telling herself she was just experiencing and taking pleasure in *touch*.

"Let's get these clothes off," he said gruffly, removing the intimate contact to hook his thumbs over the waistbands of her panties and jeans. Both garments were swiftly pushed down her legs. He lifted one of her feet, then the other, stripping them of the sandals as he also freed her of clothes.

Nicole didn't resist any of Quin's actions. Submitting to them actually kept him at a distance. She was being undressed by someone she couldn't see, being ministered to by someone she couldn't see. Now she was completely naked, yet in a strange, detached way she didn't feel vulnerable. She had a sense of liberation from all the responsibilities she had carried for so long. Right at this moment she existed only as a woman, revelling in the re-awakening of her sexuality.

His hands grazed her inner thighs as he straightened up behind her. They cupped the rounded voluptuousness of her bottom, then parted the soft cheeks enough for him to press the hard thick shaft of his erection along the cleft. Then his arms were around her waist, drawing her whole body back against his, making her acutely aware of his nakedness.

It was both strange and familiar—strange because she hadn't been with a man like this since Quin—familiar because it *was* Quin and her body recognised every inch of him. And she could not stop a wildly primitive wave of exultation in the recognition. Her man…her mate…

Except he wasn't.

Quin Sola belonged only to himself.

"What are you seeing out there?" he asked.

"Nothing," she answered, her voice sounding oddly rough, as though it was being resurrected from a long period of disuse.

"Then let me show you something to see."

He dropped his embrace, took her hand, and led her across the living room and down the hall he had entered earlier. He stopped at a door, opened it, and took her into a large bedroom. Nicole barely noticed the bed. Beyond it was another wall of glass but her gaze was not drawn to yet another view of

Sydney Harbour. It was instantly captivated by what was set up in front of the middle window.

The glass butterfly had been placed on a pedestal and spotlighted by a lamp shining up behind it and turning the wings into a stunning fluorescent blue.

CHAPTER SEVEN

No DOUBT about it, Quin thought triumphantly. As a tactic to crack Nicole's wall of indifference to him, placing the blue butterfly centre stage and spotlighting it was an act of pure genius. Gone was the submissive sex slave. She spun to face him in full frontal attack, her green eyes shooting furious sparks, outrage pumping through her, shoulders back, breasts lifting, and if her taut nipples had been pistols, there would probably be blood on the floor right now.

"What do you think you're playing at?"

Definitely a *kill* note in her voice.

"It's a beautiful piece," he stated calmly. "It should be displayed like that. Why are you upset by it?"

"You did it deliberately."

Violent accusation.

"Yes, I did," Quin agreed. "I wanted to get the best effect."

"Since when have you been interested in doing home decoration?"

Blistering scorn.

He smiled. "You inspired me to start tonight."

"Why?"

"Because it means something to you."

"No, it doesn't!" she denied heatedly, her hands clenching, her need to fight the point making Quin all the more certain he'd hit on a highly vulnerable area in her current life.

"Then it shouldn't be upsetting you, Nicole. My aim was to give you pleasure."

"Pleasure!"

The fury in her eyes whirled into confusion, followed by flickers of fear at having reacted too strongly, consequently revealing there was far more to the issue of the butterfly than she wanted him to know.

"Pleasure beyond what we share in bed," he said silkily, moving in to claim what she owed him, taking her in his embrace, ignoring the stiff resistance of her body as he pressed his to it. "It's something beautiful for you to look at tonight. And when you wake in the morning."

Her hands were still clenched at her sides. Her eyes burned with an angry hatred. There was nothing cool and detached about her now. Why she should hate him, he didn't know, but hate was infinitely better than indifference. Quin sensed she was steaming inside, wanting to lash out at him, and he exulted in having stirred so much volatile emotion. He didn't want a passive Nicole in bed. He wanted the passionate Nicole who'd left an indelible imprint on his memory.

"Bed," she bit out, pouring a mountain of venom into the word. "Right! Let's get to it!"

He laughed at her boiling impatience to get it over and done with. "Not so fast, Nicole. We haven't even kissed yet."

"Not a good idea, Quin," she flashed back at him. "I might bite your tongue out."

"I think I'll risk it anyhow."

"Whores don't kiss."

"You're no whore, Nicole. The money is totally irrelevant to what pulses between us."

"That's your ego talking, Quin. I wouldn't be here but for the money."

"Okay. Then give me my money's worth." He whipped a hand up to cup her chin, holding her face so she couldn't turn it away. "Use your tongue for something other than talking."

She opened her mouth to speak again and he swooped on it, his own passions aroused by her refusal to acknowledge the powerful chemistry between them. He kissed her hard, determined on crashing through any resistance.

There was a non-responsive moment of shock.

Then her tongue was tangling with his in a fierce duel for possession, no holding back, no sharp teeth trying to beat him into retreat. She assaulted his mouth with as much pumped up passion as he assaulted hers, and the excitement of it was so intense, Quin's entire body was seized with the need to drive it further.

Her arms had wound around his neck, hands thrust aggressively into his hair to enforce *her* kiss. It was easy to lower his hold on her, using the leverage of her lushly cushioned bottom to lift her up enough for him to stride to the bed and move them both onto it. Her legs sprawled apart invitingly as he came down on top of her. An exhilarating rush of adrenaline surged through him at the obvious proof that she wanted him as urgently as he wanted her.

Swiftly positioning himself, feeling her

moist heat, knowing she was ready, her flesh quivering, craving what he craved, Quin was on the point of plunging forward when she suddenly slammed her hands against his shoulders and cried, "No! No! Wait!"

"What for?" he snapped, every taut nerve and muscle protesting the delay, his mind angrily whirling over the thought of her playing some sadistic, teasing game with him.

"You have to use protection, Quin," she said forcefully, her breasts heaving against his chest, her knees up, feet planted to give her pushing strength if she had to use it.

"You've got some infectious problem?" His voice was harsh with frustration. Apart from which, he didn't believe that a woman as fastidious as Nicole would have taken any health risk with sex.

"How do I know *you* haven't got one?" she retaliated. "Don't tell me you've been celibate for the past five years."

"No, but I'm not stupid, Nicole."

"I want you to use a condom," she pressed aggressively.

"That's not as pleasurable for you or me."

"Tough!" Her eyes savagely mocked his argument. "Me getting pregnant is not part of our deal."

"Pregnant? You're worried about getting pregnant?"

"It happens," she said fiercely.

He frowned over the sharpness of her concern. It seemed unreasonable, given the effectiveness of modern means of contraception.

Perhaps realising it needed some credible explanation, she blurted out, "I'm not on the pill, Quin. By insisting on having me with you tonight, you didn't give me time to get myself safely protected."

His mind swiftly processed what she was saying. "So you haven't been sexually active for some time...months...years?"

Five years? he wondered, recalling her crack about the possible length of his celibacy.

"That's none of your business." Again her eyes were savagely mocking as she added, "The point is, you don't want a child out of this any more than I do. Such a responsibility would interfere far too much with your life. Though, of course, you could just turn your back on it, leaving me to deal with the consequences of our...*pleasure*."

Was that a bitter tone in her voice?

Quin forgot about the enforced pause to

their current pleasure, his mind totally engaged with Nicole's response to him on other levels. "I've never shirked responsibility," he stated, ironically conscious of the family debt he'd carried and eventually paid out. "Nor did I turn my back on you, Nicole. It was you who walked away."

"After you shut about a million doors in my face," she said derisively. "Only the bedroom door was always open. But let's not go down that road, Quin. We're dealing with now and I don't want any mementoes—butterflies or babies—of this time together. I brought a packet of condoms in case you didn't have a ready supply. It's in my bag."

The raging desire was gone. The act of getting up and doing the whole condom thing was a passion killer anyway, Quin told himself, moving to lie beside Nicole. The whole night stretched ahead of them. There was no need for any haste in satisfying the hunger for a deeply sexual connection with her. Other intimacies also had appeal.

"Shall I get the packet?" she asked, turning towards him and propping herself up on her elbow.

"Sure! Might as well be prepared for

when I get another erection," he drawled sardonically.

She glanced down and winced at the limp evidence of doused arousal. "Sorry, Quin. I should have spoken before. I didn't deliberately hold back on it."

He cocked a challenging eyebrow. "Caught up in other things?"

Her lips compressed. No admission that she'd wanted *him*. But she had. No doubt about that in Quin's mind. The triumphant knowledge of it simmered in his eyes as he said, "I put your bag in the ensuite bathroom." He waved to a door beyond the bedside table closest to where he lay. "It's through there."

It meant she had to clamber over him or get up on her side and round the bed, passing directly by the blue butterfly which he'd cunningly displayed with the only light switched on in the room. He watched her as she took the latter action. Her naked body was briefly silhouetted against the spotlight as she headed for the bathroom, her gaze rigidly fixed on the door, not so much as a glance at the butterfly.

Her lovely full breasts seemed heavier, not quite as perky as he remembered. A more mature figure five years down the track, he thought, but certainly no less sexy. To his mind, her body was still the most beautifully feminine he'd ever seen; curves where there should be curves, flowing in perfect harmony, her bones softly fleshed, long shapely legs.

He was glad she wasn't inhibited about it, feeling no need to cover up in front of him. Which would have been absurd anyway, given they'd been lovers. Nevertheless, it conceded a familiarity she might have wanted to reject in these current circumstances with hostility a strong thread in her attitude towards him.

Quin brooded over the hostility while she was out of sight in the bathroom. He didn't really understand it. When they'd first met at the bank where they'd been employed, the sexual chemistry between them had been instant and compelling. They'd both been swept away by it. There'd been no courtship. One dinner date followed by blazing passion. It had taken enormous discipline for him not to become obsessed with her, not to lose sight of the goal he'd set himself.

Despite the cost to the financial momentum he'd been building, he'd moved out of his mother's home and rented an apartment so he and Nicole could be together as much as possible. Nicole had been happy with the arrangement. The sexual excitement had been intense and they were also highly compatible out of bed, with her understanding the pressures of trading and his being able to converse knowingly about her work in sales.

She was the only woman he'd ever lived with, the only one he'd ever wanted to live with. Being with her had always been an enormous buzz. It still was. But in the end she hadn't been satisfied with what they had.

He couldn't remember when she'd started agitating about meeting each other's families. He hadn't wanted to go there. It meant getting more tied up with Nicole than he already was and he didn't want to think about future relationships when he hadn't yet discharged the burden of the past. One thing at a time. He'd been adamant about simply continuing to share what they did— just the two of them—which didn't have anything to do with their families.

He had sensed an emotional withdrawal from her—a coldness stemming, he'd thought, from not getting her own way. He hadn't fallen in with her design for their lives, whatever that was—marriage, babies, setting up a family home. Nevertheless, she had seemed to accept that he wasn't about to change his mind—remaining with him for two years before deciding to break off their relationship and go overseas.

He recalled her bitter claim that making money had been more important to him than she was. To Quin's mind, the two things should not have been in conflict. Both had been important to him. But she had gone, deliberately putting so much distance between them, it wrote off any second chance with her, and since that was her choice…why did she now hate him?

Had she wanted him—expected him—to drop everything and chase after her?

He'd missed her. He'd missed her one hell of a lot. But he'd had a job to do, a vow to fulfil, and he'd driven himself to carry it through and have done with it. He was free now. His mother was back home in Argentina, welcomed into her family circle again. She'd wanted him to stay, too, but the life there had no appeal to him. Australia had become his home country.

Having returned to Sydney and established his own business, he had been feeling the need for someone to share his life with. He'd tried several attractive women, all of them falling short of satisfying him in one area or another. He hadn't been consciously comparing them to Nicole, yet the moment he'd seen her again, he knew she was the one he had to have.

She emerged from the bathroom, coming straight to his side of the bed and handing him the packet of condoms. "You might as well get one out ready," she said, her green eyes glittering determined purpose as she moved to sit astride him, intent on arousing his flesh with her own.

"I did mention there was no hurry, Nicole," he reminded her, though he proceeded to extract the contraceptive device, wanting it ready when he chose to use it. "I'm happy just to talk for a while."

"Then talk away," she answered carelessly, moving her lower body over his in tantalising provocation.

She looked magnificent sitting there on top of him, her breasts swaying to the voluptuous roll of her hips, her long curly hair a cloud of sensual promise, shimmering against the backdrop of the spotlighted blue butterfly.

Had she positioned herself like this so it

was behind her, out of her line of sight? "I'm glad you want to make love to me," he said as a goad to revealing her thoughts.

She flicked him a veiled look, her thick lashes almost hiding—but not quite—the hot daggers behind them. "I might just be satisfying myself."

"Then I'm glad to be of service to you."

She raked her nails lightly down his chest, not scratching but possibly delivering a warning that the claws could be unsheathed if he pushed her too far.

Quin rather relished flirting with danger. "How long has it been since you were with a man, Nicole?" he asked, wanting his curiosity satisfied on that point. If there'd been no other since she'd left him…

"Obviously I've been occupied by other things," she tossed out as though he should have realised that from the situation she had already laid out to him.

"Even as far back as two years ago?"

It stilled her for a moment. But she was quick at making the connection. "Your friend, Tony Fisher, is not as irresistible as he might think he is."

"Most women find Tony very attractive."

"Guess it's a matter of personal taste." Her

eyes flashed derisively as she bent forward to kiss one of his nipples, swirling her tongue around it and sucking on it as though revelling in its taste.

If it was meant to be a powerful distraction from any further conversation, it certainly hit its mark. The sheer physical excitement of it tested his control to its limits. Only the thought that she was winning gave him the will power to remain still and keep his brain working, though he didn't realise his breath was trapped in his chest until she lifted her mouth away. He quickly exhaled and gulped in more air as her head moved towards his other nipple.

"Did you find satisfaction in London?" he shot out, trying to pinpoint how she'd spent the years of her absence overseas.

She ignored the question, delivering the same sweet torment again, driving the desire to subject *her* to it until her whole body ached for the release he could give her, until she was begging for it. He had twenty-five more nights for talking. It could wait. This couldn't. Not even for one more second.

He grabbed her waist, hurled her onto her back, rolled to pin her down under his weight. She tore at his hair as he swooped on her breasts. She kneaded his shoulders when he pushed himself down to wrap his mouth around more intimate places. Her body bucked, writhed and finally she did beg.

For a moment he hesitated over donning the condom.

If Nicole did get pregnant and had his child, she'd be tied to him for life.

But that wouldn't be a free choice.

He wanted her to want him in her life.

And he didn't want to be stopped now.

So the protective sheath had to be used.

She climaxed as he drove his triumphant possession of her as deeply as he could go, but that wasn't enough for Quin. He was consumed with the burning desire to feel her coming again and again, rolling from one ecstatic peak to the next. He wanted to drive the memory of any other lover she'd had right out of her mind so she remembered only him. He used every bit of sexual expertise he knew to keep her body tuned to his, responding instinctively, blissfully, lustfully, lovingly, long into the night.

As she had in the past.

Oh, yes, he wanted that back.

And more!

CHAPTER EIGHT

IT WAS the twelfth night coming up. Almost halfway through the deal, Nicole told herself, trying to quell the growing sense that she would never really be free of Joaquin Luis Sola. He was like a drug. The more she had of him, the more she wanted him. Just like before. And labelling what they had together, *just sex*, did not lessen the impact of it. Walking away from him a second time was not going to be any easier than the first.

She stared at the reflection of her eyes in the bathroom mirror. They literally glittered with excitement, all because she could tell him tonight they didn't have to use condoms anymore. She'd now been taking the pill long enough for it to be effective. They didn't have to think about protection, didn't have to stop, didn't have to blunt the feeling of absolutely natural intimacy.

She couldn't even pretend her skin was tingling from the brisk towelling she'd given it after her shower. Her whole body was anticipating his touch. And here she was blow-drying her freshly shampooed hair so it would look good for him, feel good to him, silky and sensual and...

"Nicole..." Her mother called out, knocking on the bathroom door to gain her attention. "You're wanted on the 'phone."

"Coming..." She quickly switched off the hair drier, laid it on the vanity bench, then grabbed her bathrobe and wrapped it around the nakedness she hadn't bothered to cover before, secretly revelling in a sense of wanton expectation. She opened the door to find her mother still loitering in the hall, watching for her to emerge. "Who is it?" Nicole asked, wondering why she appeared anxious.

Linda Ellis looked at the happy glow emanating from her daughter and felt her own heart tighten with concern. That same aura of happiness had been totally blighted by the man Nicole had picked up with again. If that happened a second time, it would be completely her fault for not ever having stopped to count the cost of trying to save Harry. A futile sacrifice in the end. And this sacrifice by Nicole could also end in wretched grief.

"It's him," she said flatly.

"You mean Quin?" Nicole asked, the sparkle in her eyes disappearing under a sudden cloud of worry.

Linda nodded.

Frowning heavily, Nicole hurried down the hall to the kitchen where the house telephone resided. Linda trailed after her, disturbed by this direct contact with the man who had never wanted to meet her, never wanted anything to do with Nicole's family. She propped herself in the kitchen doorway, needing to eavesdrop on the call, needing to know where all this might be leading

Nicole snatched up the telephone receiver which had been left waiting for her on the kitchen bench. Her heart was racing, her stomach fluttering. "How did you get this number?" she demanded, the fear of Quin encroaching on her real life shooting through her mind.

"I looked it up in the telephone book," he answered matter-of-factly.

"It's in my mother's name," she snapped back.

"The same name, Linda Ellis, attached to the debts I paid off, including the mortgage on a house in Burwood," he drawled.

Nicole paused to take a deep, calming breath and to get her wits in order. Of course Quin had enough information to find her. The question was…why bother? He never had before.

"Calling me at home is not in our deal," she stated pointedly.

"I am calling out of consideration for you, Nicole. I didn't think you'd like coming to my apartment tonight and not finding me there."

Not there tonight? The sexual excitement she had been trying to contain all day took a dive into disappointment. Anger at herself stirred. She was letting Quin get to her far too much. A determination to halt that process put a coolness in her voice.

"Thank you for letting me know you're forfeiting the twelfth night of our deal in favour of something else."

"I have no intention of forfeiting any night," he whipped back.

"You just have, Quin."

"I'll be home tomorrow. A mere postponement."

"We made the arrangement—Fridays and Mondays. I'm not available to you on any other nights."

"Be reasonable, Nicole." His voice was very terse now. "I'm in Melbourne. A business meeting ran over and—"

"And, as always, making money comes ahead of being with me," she cut in bitingly. "That's fine, Quin. Your choice. But don't expect me to accommodate your choice."

She could hear him exhale a long breath of exasperation at her refusal to oblige him. Nicole felt pleased with herself for not giving in to him. *Score one for me,* she thought, remembering how she'd done whatever was needed to fit around his work in the past.

However, her moment of grim satisfaction was abruptly ended by Zoe rushing in from the living room, calling, "Mummy! Mummy! Come and see what's on television."

Nicole swung around from the kitchen

bench, caught sight of her mother in the doorway and shot her a wildly pleading look.

Zoe was swiftly scooped up in her grandmother's arms. "I'll come and look," she was assured and carried back into the living room.

"But I want…"

"Shh…"

The door was shut behind them, keeping them both out of earshot.

Nicole was gripped by shock, the childish voice of her daughter still ringing in her ears as she fearfully wondered if Quin had heard it. The suspended beating of her heart broke into an erratic pounding when he spoke again.

"Mummy?" The puzzled query was followed by a sharper question. "Whose child was that, Nicole?"

Her mind wrenched itself out of its distressed daze and flew to desperate defence stations. "The daughter of one of my friends. They dropped by to—" she deliberately huffed over the lie before adding "—but that's none of your business, Quin. Thank you for calling to warn me tonight is off. Is Friday night a firm date or can I expect another cancellation?"

He huffed. Or rather a long heated breath hissed through his teeth. "You'll be seeing me," he said curtly, and ended the connection.

Nicole fumbled the receiver back onto its holder and sagged against the bench. That was too close a call. The relief of having come up with a swift explanation for Zoe's presence still had her trembling inside.

It hadn't occurred to her that Quin might contact her at home. He never had in the past. But then they'd been living together and working for the same bank. When she'd visited her mother, he had viewed it as time out from their relationship and didn't intrude on it.

This was a different situation and she could hardly criticise Quin for giving her a courtesy call. She should have been more prepared for possible glitches in their arrangement. Although he had her e-mail address, e-mailing was not an immediate means of communication unless one was sitting at the computer all the time. And she would not have logged on before leaving this evening.

Shame wormed through her as she thought of how fixated her mind had been on having sex with Quin. He was starting to dominate her life again and she had to protect herself from that. Fourteen more nights…what if she didn't want to end it?

Nicole shook her head angrily. That was crazy thinking. Right now she was caught up in indulging her sexuality. Quin was good for that but not for anything else. If she didn't keep everything in perspective she'd be in bad trouble. And right now Zoe needed her attention.

She quickly entered the living room to find her daughter sitting on Nanna's lap, placidly watching "The World Around Us" program on television—no apparent upset at having been ignored by her mother. Nicole paused for a moment, taking in the two people who did occupy the central core of her life.

They personified love, not lust. Without her mother's ready support, Nicole knew she could not have managed the period of Zoe's illness nearly as well. Then for Harry to have been hit by cancer… Nicole could not begrudge the extreme lengths her mother had gone to in search of a cure. It had been done out of love. And it had to be very hard to lose two husbands. Losing out on Quin's love had devastated her five years ago.

We three are the survivors, Nicole thought, *three generations of the one small family.*

In the past few weeks her mother had pulled herself together and was back managing the dance school. The grey had been dyed out of her short curly brown hair and her trim dancer's body and still pretty face belied her fifty-five years. Occasionally Nicole glimpsed a haunted look in the generally warm hazel eyes, but at least the depression that had followed Harry's death had lifted.

As for Zoe, she was always a delight—a wonderfully healthy delight—and to Nicole's mind, the most beautiful little girl in the world with her large smoky grey eyes and the amazingly thick, glossy, black hair which Zoe wanted to grow long so it could be braided. Nicole was smiling over this ambitious aim as she walked over to the three-seater sofa facing the television screen.

"You missed it, Mummy," Zoe informed her, heaving a disappointed sigh.

"I'm sorry, darling. I was busy on the 'phone and couldn't cut off the person calling me." She sat down beside her daughter, smiling encouragingly. "Tell me what you saw."

Her little face lit up with awe. "It was a butterfly farm."

"An enclosure, like an aviary," Nanna supplied.

"And there were lots and lots of big pretty flowers for the butterflies to land on."

"Tropical flowers," Nanna chimed in. "Most of them hibiscus."

"It was near the rainforest at Kranda. Could we go there, Mummy?"

"Kuranda," Nanna corrected. "Up above Cairns in Far North Queensland."

Nicole shook her head. "That's too far away, Zoe. It was lucky you saw it on TV."

Zoe heaved a sigh but didn't argue. She knew only too well that some things could be done and some things couldn't. "They were all blue, the butterflies. The man called them—" she frowned, trying to recall the word "—Issies."

"Ulysses," Nicole recollected with painful irony. The glass one Quin had bought was still prominently displayed in his bedroom— a tormenting reminder of what he didn't know, what he wouldn't want to know.

Zoe cocked her head appealingly. "If we can't go and see them, could you make one for my tree, Mummy? We haven't got a blue one. Not all blue like the Ulysses."

Nicole inwardly winced, knowing it would be forever connected to her nights with Quin. "Butterflies mark special occasions, Zoe. You'll have to wait for one," she said, hoping her daughter might forget about the blue Ulysses. "Now I must go finish drying my hair before I tuck you into bed for the night. Okay?"

"Okay, Mummy."

Nicole caught a frown from her mother, worry in the hazel eyes. "Are you…going out?" she asked warily.

"No. I just want to finish doing my hair or it will end up frizzy," Nicole rattled off carelessly, hoping to dismiss anything her mother had overheard from the kitchen doorway.

However, after she'd put Zoe to bed and read her a story, she found her mother pacing around the living room in an agitated state, the television switched off. "What's wrong, Mum? You're missing your favourite crime show."

"I don't like this, Nicole," was shot back at her. "On the 'phone to that man, you sounded so bitter…vengeful." She wrung her hands. "It's wrong, wrong. I shouldn't have let you do this."

"You didn't let me, Mum. I did it on my own. *My* choice," Nicole insisted quietly.

"It's not good for you."

"Oh, I don't know. In a weird kind of way it is."

"How?"

Nicole managed a wry smile. "I doubt there's a man alive who's as good as Quin in bed. It's not exactly a hardship to spend twenty-six nights with him."

"Do you still love him?"

"No."

"I don't believe you can have really good sex without loving your partner," her mother argued heatedly.

Nicole tried to shrug off the point. "Well, Quin and I still have a strong physical connection. It's okay, Mum. Don't worry about it."

"No, it's more than that. You're getting hurt by him again. I heard it in your voice. You can't change people, Nicole. They are what they are. And paying them back for not living up to what you want of them…"

"It's not about what I want," Nicole cut in fiercely. "Quin and I have a deal. A deal is a deal. No changes. That was all I was insisting upon, Mum. Now please…leave it alone.

I do not wish to spend any more of my time on Quin than what he's paid for."

But, of course she did. He was on her mind more often than not. Her mother respected her wishes enough to drop the subject for the time being but her silence didn't stop Nicole from thinking about him, nor brooding over what her mother had said.

When they both retired for the night, Nicole lay awake and very acutely alone in her own bed, hashing over what she did feel about Quin Sola. The bottom line was she did wish he would change and her bitterness stemmed from having her wishes thwarted. Her mother was right. Being vengeful did not bring about some magical transformation. On the other hand, it did satisfy a dark sense of justice to belittle his role in her life, as he had belittled hers when she'd desperately needed something else from him.

There was no good answer to any of this, she finally decided, and set her mind to counting sheep in the hope it would send her to sleep. It must have succeeded because she was jerked awake by the loud and persistent ringing of the doorbell.

She looked at her bedside clock: 23:17. Was the house on fire or something? She sniffed but didn't smell any smoke. Nevertheless, there had to be an emergency to account for such determination to arouse the people in the house. She tumbled out of bed and met her mother in the hall heading for the front door. She stopped as she heard Zoe calling out, alarmed by the bell which was still being rung aggressively.

Not for one second did it occur to Nicole that Quin Sola might be at the door, that a determination not to forfeit one night with her had caused him to cut his business meeting short, catch a plane from Melbourne to Sydney and come to this house in Burwood to collect her before midnight!

CHAPTER NINE

HAVING jettisoned his plans and travelled hard for the past few hours to get here, Quin was not a happy man to find the house in darkness. It was an old but solid red brick Federation-style home with a neat front lawn and garden—typical of the whole street—yet with no light on anywhere, its old-fashioned respectability felt forbidding. Definitely unwelcoming.

And this was the house he'd saved for her!

So what had Nicole done, having thrown down her challenge about his priorities? Gone out with her mother for the night? Taken herself off to a bed that didn't have him in it? She certainly hadn't been waiting around to see if he'd turn up. Which made Quin fighting mad. She wanted the deal kept to the letter, then let her keep it, too. Tonight she had to be available to him!

The worst of it was he'd thought she'd been softening towards him, actively wanting to spend time together, enjoying their nights. He'd believed he'd been making headway towards drawing her into the same close relationship they'd had before. Tonight it had struck him forcibly that he now had more than enough money to do anything he wanted, and what he wanted most was Nicole Ashton. It didn't matter if he lost a lucrative client. It did matter if he lost Nicole again.

If she needed a demonstration of how important she was to him, fine…but it wasn't fine to have his demonstration shown up as totally irrelevant to her. A fierce resentment put a savage twist to his ringing of the doorbell, which was an old-style metal mechanism, not a modern button, and much more satisfying to operate—snapping it back and forth, back and forth. However, the loud clanging seemed to echo through an empty house, which drove his frustration higher.

If Nicole had gone out, he'd camp on this porch until she returned and insist she make up the time he'd been kept waiting. His gaze skated around, looking for a chair. No chair. But in the far corner…a doll's pram? Must have been overlooked and left behind by the friend who had the little girl.

His hand was still working the bell when light suddenly shone through the glass panels of the door. So someone was at home! He kept the loud ringing going to encourage a fast response to it. The blurred image of a woman appeared behind the stained glass. The door rattled as it was hastily unlocked. Quin dropped his hand to his side and composed himself to confront Nicole with his refusal to forfeit.

The door opened.

The woman facing him was not Nicole.

She had short hair and was middle-aged. Her dressing-gown had not been properly adjusted and her hair was mussed—clear indications that she'd been disturbed from sleep. Her initial expression of confused alarm changed to sharp annoyance as he simply stared at her, coming to the realisation that this had to be Nicole's mother, Linda Ellis.

"Who are you? What's the problem?" she rapped out.

He looked her straight in the eye and said, "My name is Quin Sola and I have business with your daughter, Mrs Ellis."

"You!" It was a gasp of shock. In the next instant her whole body was recoiling from him as though he was the worst possible news.

Quin frowned over the reaction. Although they'd never met, Linda Ellis certainly knew his name and obviously it didn't conjure up good feelings. Which raised the question…what had Nicole been telling her about him? Didn't being rescued from financial ruin give her mother cause enough to be more welcoming towards her benefactor?

"Is Nicole here?" he asked, deciding quite a few things needed to be confronted and settled in this household.

Linda Ellis didn't answer.

She didn't have to answer.

Over her shoulder he caught sight of Nicole stepping into the hall from a room at the back of it. She carried a child, a little girl whose head was snuggled into the curve of her neck and shoulder. Both of them were wrapped in hurriedly donned dressing-gowns.

"What is it, Mum?"

The words had tripped off Nicole's tongue before she saw him. When her mother stepped back to reveal his presence and recognition hit, her forward momentum along the hall came to a dead halt, shock radiating from her frozen stillness.

The little girl lifted her head and looked directly at Quin, wanting to find a reason for the sudden stop, the silence. She had short black hair, cut in a bob. Her large and thickly lashed eyes were surprisingly light—a smoky grey—and Quin thought there was something familiar about her face, but...

"Do you know this man, Mummy?" the child asked.

Mummy!

Quin's gaze jerked to Nicole's. Anguish in her eyes now, not shock. A flood of heat turned her cheeks scarlet. Her throat moved convulsively, swallowing hard, needing words to emerge from it but not finding them easy to form. Her chin lifted, signalling defiant pride before she finally spoke.

"He's just someone passing by, Zoe." This relegation to insignificant status in her life was accompanied by a glare that rejected any other possibility in the future. "Please excuse me while I put my daughter back to bed."

The child looked curiously at him over her mother's shoulder as Nicole wheeled and headed back down the hall. There was something about the little girl's eyes, her face...the odd familiarity niggled past the stunning fact of her existence in Nicole's life. His mind almost burst with the intuitive leap that speared through it.

My child!

Certainty gripped him as he judged the little girl to be about four years old. Mother and daughter disappeared from view, re-entering the room from which they had emerged. He switched his attention to Linda Ellis, his eyes boring into hers for the truth.

"She's mine, isn't she? *My* child!"

Her hand lifted to her throat as though instinctively moving to choke off any admission. She shook her head in frightened agitation. To Quin's mind there was no reason for fear unless the connection was true and the plan was to keep him in ignorance. *As they had for the past five years!*

He brushed past Nicole's mother and charged down the hall, the need to have his certainty absolutely confirmed pumping through him. The door to the bedroom had been left slightly ajar. He pushed it open.

The overhead light was still on and Quin was momentarily distracted by the startling vision of the butterfly tree, set in front of a bay window, its long, twisted, greyish white driftwood branches loaded with dozens of beautiful butterflies in all sizes and colours. A wonderful decoration for a little girl's room, he thought, wrenching his gaze away from its fascination to target the mother and child who'd just flipped his life into another dimension.

Nicole was by the bed, bent over in the act of removing the little girl's dressing-gown, blocking him off from her daughter—*their* daughter. The urge to stake a claim here and now was far too strong for Quin to deny.

"Your mother is mistaken, Zoe," he said.

Nicole straightened up and whipped around, shooting him a killer look for intruding on what she considered her territory.

Not just hers any more, he silently resolved, strolling forward, his gaze fastened on the child who was so clearly flesh of his flesh, blood of his blood. *She* was not frightened of him, not his daughter. She stood her ground, looking gravely at him, waiting to hear what the mistake was, and Quin was flooded by a tumultuous mix of emotions—wonder, pride, tenderness, a fierce need to protect, the desire to hold her close, hug her tight.

But he was a stranger to her and restraint was called for until she accepted him for who he was. He squatted down to speak to her at eye level. "I'm not just someone passing by," he explained. "I've been away for a long time. All your life so far. But I aim to stay around for the rest of it."

"Quin!" The grated protest from Nicole drew Zoe's attention to her.

"That's my name," he quickly said, offering a smile that promised he was harmless. It persuaded their daughter into looking directly at him again. "My full name is Joaquin Luis Sola, but most people, like your mother, call me Quin for short. I'm very, very glad to meet you, Zoe."

He offered his hand.

She glanced up at her mother for instruction but none was forthcoming. Quin could feel Nicole staring at him—huge tension emanating from her—but he kept his concentration focused on Zoe, willing her to respond to him.

Her gaze dropped to his hand. After a long, breathless moment, she tentatively offered hers. Quin couldn't help grinning in happy triumph as he took it. Her sweetly curved mouth—Nicole's mouth—returned a shy smile.

"Hello," he said encouragingly, loving the soft warmth of her little hand in his.

"Hello," she returned, her eyes locked onto his, wanting to know more of him.

And the words simply spilled out of Quin.

"I'm your daddy."

CHAPTER TEN

NICOLE's mind was jammed with so many conflicting thoughts it was impossible to produce any sensible response to Quin's declaration. She listened dumbly as Zoe started her own childish interrogation, trying to understand where Quin was coming from, why he was here now.

"My daddy?" she queried wonderingly.

"Yes," Quin confirmed, admitting no doubt whatsoever. "Look for yourself," he invited. "We have the same eyes, the same hair, the same nose. I'm your father."

Silence while she studied the face in front of her. Then she looked up at Nicole for assurance. "Is it true, Mummy?"

Nicole's head ached from the terrible mental traffic racing through it. Her heart was squeezed by so many painful emotions, it struggled to keep beating. Her mouth was hopelessly dry. "Yes," she croaked out, realising it would be futile to deny it.

Zoe returned her gaze to the father who had been missing all her life and with artless innocence asked, "Where have you been, Daddy? Why have you come now in the middle of the night?"

Quin didn't even pause to think. He came straight out with, "I've been lost in another world to yours, Zoe. And I've only just found my way here. I couldn't wait until tomorrow to see you. I hope you don't mind."

Magnetic charm was pouring out of him.

And Nicole hated him for it.

Winning over their daughter when he hadn't paid a moment's pain for her wasn't fair. Nowhere near fair.

"Will you be here tomorrow?" Zoe asked.

"That depends on whether your mother will let me stay," he answered.

"Mummy?" A look of appeal from Zoe.

"We mustn't count on it," she warned her daughter before shooting a fuming look at Quin. "Your father might have to go back to his other world."

"Do you have to, Daddy?" Zoe asked directly.

"Not if I can help it, but your mother and

I need to talk about how we can be together. If I'm not here tomorrow, I promise I'll be back very soon. Okay?"

He smiled at her.

She smiled back, believing him. "Okay."

"Back to sleep now," Nicole commanded, unable to bear any more togetherness between Quin and her daughter. She lifted Zoe into bed and tucked her up tightly, wanting to shield her precious child from the man who could make a terrible mess of their lives.

"Good night, darling," she murmured, pressing a fervent kiss on her forehead—a kiss of love that spanned years, not a few minutes.

"'Night, Mummy. Is my Daddy going to kiss me goodnight, too?"

"Yes, he is," Quin asserted before Nicole could reply, and she had to stand back and let him do it, fighting a mountain of fierce resentment at his assumption of a role he hadn't earned.

She closed her ears to the all too intimate murmurs between them and walked to the door, impatient to usher Quin out, get him away from her daughter.

He came promptly enough not to stir her anger any higher, glancing at the butterfly tree before he passed out of the room. She switched off the light, closed the door, and led off to the kitchen which was far enough away from Zoe for a private conversation to be held without any risk of disturbing her.

The smell of newly made hot chocolate—a comfort drink—indicated that her mother was still up, anxiously waiting to be cued about what to do next. She burst into fearful speech the moment Nicole entered the kitchen.

"I didn't tell him, Nicole. He guessed."

"It's not your fault, Mum. It's mine for not agreeing to a postponement. He came to claim his night." Acutely aware of the man just behind her, she turned to shoot him a derisive look. "Right, Quin?"

"Right!" he agreed ironically.

"But it is my fault!" her mother cried, looking hopelessly wretched about the situation. "If I hadn't got so deeply in debt, you would never have gone to him, never…"

"Wrong, Mrs. Ellis," Quin cut in strongly, moving up to stand beside Nicole. "The moment I saw Nicole again, I was determined to get her back in my life one way or another. Your debt was simply a means to the end I wanted."

The ruthless purpose in his voice sent a

convulsive shiver down Nicole's spine. Would he now *use* Zoe to keep her sexually tied to him?

Her mother looked distractedly at Quin, not understanding the strict parameters attached to his idea of a relationship. "Why? It's not fair!" she cried. "You didn't want my daughter enough to marry her when it counted."

"At the time, I didn't know how much it counted, Mrs. Ellis," he replied in a tone of quiet gravity.

Didn't *want* to know, Nicole thought.

"You carry no blame for anything to do with me and Zoe, Mum," she quickly asserted. "You've been wonderfully supportive all along. So please don't fret over this. It's up to me to sort it out with Quin. If you'll just leave us alone…"

Her mother heaved a ragged sigh, rubbed her forehead in agitation, then picked up her mug of hot chocolate and moved to leave the kitchen, looking totally dispirited.

Quin spoke. "This probably won't mean much to you, Mrs Ellis, but I'm sorry I wasn't here for Nicole and Zoe, and I thank you very sincerely for supporting them throughout my absence."

She stopped beside him, looked sharply

into his eyes, shook her head as though the situation was completely beyond her, then walked off without another word, heading for her bedroom.

Nicole moved briskly to the refrigerator, intending to get out the milk to make a hot comfort drink for herself *and* gain some fighting distance from Quin. When her mother's bedroom door closed loudly enough to punctuate their privacy in the kitchen she turned on him, spitting mad.

"Sorry? You aren't sorry about one damned thing, Quin! Nothing was ever going to stop you from doing what you wanted. Not back then. And not now, either. You just don't care how *what you want* affects other people."

He was still just inside the kitchen, his immobility radiating the air of a powerful animal, watching and waiting for the moment to move into attack. "I would have made adjustments if you'd told me you were pregnant, Nicole," he stated unequivocally, his eyes burning that truth into hers.

She glared her own truth straight back at him. "You didn't make any for me, Quin."

"I did, actually." His mouth twisted with

irony. "It cost me quite a bit to set up an apartment so we could live together."

"Money!" she retorted with blistering scorn.

"Money that wouldn't have been spent, but for you."

"Because you *wanted* me."

"And I would have wanted our daughter, too," he returned as quick as a whip.

"Well, I chose for us not to be your possessions, Quin," she flashed back at him. "That was all I was to you, and all our daughter would have been, too. Possessions you had to pay for."

In a fury of resentment she jerked the refrigerator door open, removed the bottle of milk, slammed the door shut, turned to the sink, got a mug from the overhead cupboard and started spooning in chocolate powder from the tin her mother had left on the bench. Her hands were shaking.

"I'm sorry I made you feel that."

She gritted her teeth. No way would she let the soft tone of his apology get to her. Empty words. All too easy to say when the past was the distant past. She willed her hands to be steady for pouring the milk over the chocolate powder.

"I thought we were two single adults, making careers for ourselves, and lucky enough to have something good and mutual going," he added ruefully, then had the hide to say, "I was as much your possession as you were mine, Nicole."

She swung around to shoot him down. "Only when we shared a bed! Out of it you had your own agenda, which possessed you far more strongly than I ever did." Her eyes stabbed any possible protest from him. "Don't deny it, Quin. I lived with how it was for you. And how it was for me. I know."

His face visibly tightened at the hit.

He said nothing.

She turned back to shove the mug into the microwave and set the timer. The seconds on the digital clock started ticking down. It was a terribly slow countdown compared to the galloping beat of her heart, but she watched it obsessively, willing time away because she wasn't ready to face what Quin's knowledge of Zoe might mean to their lives.

"If you don't want me in your life, Nicole," he said slowly, quietly, "why did you risk coming to me that night in The Havana Club?"

"To make you pay," she blurted out.

"Pay for what? I never did anything to you that you didn't want."

"It was what you didn't do," she muttered fiercely, then braced herself to swing around and directly argue her case. "I used the sex, which was all you wanted me for, to pay for this roof over our heads, to pay for the dance school to keep going so it could support us. So you've done your paternal duty, Quin. You don't have to put yourself out to be *a father* to Zoe. We can manage just fine without you."

The timer on the microwave beeped.

Quin's gaze was locked on hers and she could feel him gearing up to use every atom of power he had to fight the position she'd just taken. It had better not be just pride driving him, she thought savagely. Zoe would be expecting more than that from her new *daddy*.

"I guess I deserve that," he said, finally acknowledging he had put limitations on their relationship in the past.

Unaccountably a rush of tears blurred her eyes. Rather than let him see them, she swiftly turned to the microwave oven, taking out the mug of steaming hot chocolate and nursing it in her trembling hands.

"But the punishment for my crimes of omission stops here, Nicole." The ruthless determination in his voice battered her frayed defences. "I didn't come tonight to claim what you owe me. I came to prove that being with you was more important than anything else. To show that I didn't want to miss any minute that you would grant me." Then more softly, "To make it different for you this time."

She shook her head, desperately trying to ignore the painful strike at her heart. "I don't believe you've changed, Quin."

"The circumstances have changed."

A bubble of hysteria burst through her brain with the recognition of how drastically they had changed. "Yes, you've found out you have a daughter. And you've put your foot into fatherhood before thinking of what that might mean to a little girl who doesn't know any better than to believe you."

"I won't give her any reason not to believe me," he blasted back without a moment's hesitation.

Anger spurted through her, stiffening her spine and putting a stop to her shakiness. She banged the mug down on the sink and spun to face him, flinging out a mocking gesture as she cried, "Oh sure! Daddy will be on hand whenever Zoe wants him, not just when Daddy finds it convenient to him."

He cut straight through her blistering sarcasm to the heart of the issue. "She wants me on hand tomorrow. Are you prepared to let that happen, Nicole, or isn't it convenient for you?"

The challenge blazing from his eyes allowed her no room to protest the arrangement. If she didn't concede, she was the one keeping *Daddy* away. "It will have to be the morning then," she said belligerently, knowing it would take time off his precious money-making. "Zoe comes with me to the dance school in the afternoon and we stay there until quite late."

"Expect me at seven o'clock tomorrow morning. I presume our daughter is awake by then." He gave her a curt nod and turned towards the hall.

"You're not staying to take your pound of flesh tonight?" she hurled after him, stunned by his decision to leave her now and to return first thing in the morning for Zoe.

He paused in the kitchen doorway and subjected her to a long searing look. "I only ever took what you gave, Nicole," he said quietly. "Perhaps you could start remembering that."

She stared at the empty space he left, listening to him walking down the hall, letting himself out of the house, closing the front door behind him. Everything inside her was aching with a sense of emptiness.

Quin didn't want her tonight.

But she still wanted him.

And it hurt—it really hurt—that he'd spurned the deal they had made.

She was not in control of anything anymore.

Had she ever been in control with Quin or had she simply been deceiving herself, using the deal as an excuse for taking what only he had ever given her?

Now, with their daughter known to him… was everything going to change?

Nicole pushed herself to walk down the hall and lock the front door. Tomorrow morning she would have to unlock it again and let Quin walk into Zoe's life.

He'd better not break her daughter's heart.

She could never forgive him that.

Never!

CHAPTER ELEVEN

Quin arrived at the Burwood house ahead of time. The early morning traffic had not been as heavy as he had anticipated and he'd been lucky in getting green lights most of the way out of the city centre. Having parked his Audi at the kerb of the suburban street, he remained in the driver's seat, waiting out the minutes before seven o'clock.

Being early would not endear him to Nicole. Given her bitter view of how he'd conducted himself with her in the past, Quin wasn't sure anything was going to endear him to Nicole. Even so, no way would he give up the battle to win her over to his presence in her life, especially now with their daughter in the picture.

Zoe…

Four years he'd missed. And the pregnancy. All because the timing had been wrong for taking his relationship with Nicole beyond immediate needs. He hadn't meant to belittle her place in his life, and he understood why she had felt no deep commitment coming from him, but having his child without his knowledge…that was so big a hit at the kind of man he was, Quin was still trying to come to terms with it.

First and foremost he was a man of honour.

He would have stood by Nicole.

But clearly she hadn't wanted him to, preferring to be on her own, to raise their child without him at her side.

That had to change. He would make it change. The big question was…how best to do it?

He checked his watch. Almost seven o'clock. He picked up the bag containing the blue butterfly from the passenger seat, alighted from the car, locked it and headed for the house, determined on making a positive impact on his daughter's life. Hopefully that might influence Nicole into viewing him with less hostility.

The front door opened just as he reached the porch. Nicole quickly stepped outside, pulling the door closed behind her—an action which instantly signalled her reluctance to let him into the house. Quin halted, observing her keenly as he waited for her to state what this move meant.

Her lovely green eyes were dull with fatigue. Not much sleep, if any, Quin thought. Her long curly hair had been brushed and her general appearance—T-shirt, jeans, sandals—was neat and tidy, but her face was nude of make-up and her skin looked pale and drawn, the strain of having to confront him this morning all too visible.

She stared too long without saying a word and he knew she was seeing him as belonging to a different world in his grey business suit. He sensed it represented pain to her and she didn't want to be anywhere near it again. The problem was they had obviously been at different places in their lives five years ago and she had nursed expectations of him which he hadn't met.

"I'm not in that place anymore, Nicole," he said impulsively, hoping to ease her stress. "I do have to go to work today. I have a business to run, just as you have a dance school to run with your mother. But I no longer have a pressing need to make as much money as I can in as little time as possible. I now have a different perspective on what I want in my life."

She shook her head, a tired disbelief in her eyes. "I realise Zoe came as a shock to you, Quin. You reacted to it without thinking through how much a commitment father-hood would be." Her mouth moved stiffly into a wry grimace as she amended her words. "Should be."

"I don't have to think it through, Nicole. We're not talking about a proposition here. Zoe is a reality."

"She doesn't have to be," came the swift, anxious rejoinder. "I could explain last night away as a dream. She's not awake yet. You could leave and let me handle all the parent-ing."

"No!" Steel shot down his backbone. Every muscle tensed in fighting mode. "I won't be wiped out of my daughter's life."

"That's ego talking, Quin, not love." Her eyes searched his in frantic concern. "I don't think you know what love is, and it's not fair to tug on a little girl's heart, then leave it empty of what she'll want from you." Her hands lifted in urgent appeal. "Please…take the time to think about it. At least, leave the decision until I come to you on Friday night."

"Waiting won't make any difference to my decision. You agreed to my coming here this morning, Nicole. I'm not going away."

"I wasn't thinking straight last night."

"Well, I was. And I'm thinking straight this morning, too." He checked his watch. "It's past seven and while you're not delighted to see me, I think my daughter will be, so can we stop this futile argument now and keep to the agreement?"

She looked at him with an angry mixture of fear and frustration. "You don't care, do you? It has to be your way or no way."

"Was your way so good, Nicole?" he countered. "Keeping Zoe to yourself? Not caring if she might want her father?"

Hot colour raced into her pale cheeks. "You weren't good for *me,* Quin. Why would I believe…"

"Yes, I was," he cut in vehemently. "I *was* good for you or you wouldn't have lived with me for so long. I just wouldn't dance to your strings and I'm not going to dance to them now, either."

He took a step closer to her, his whole body emanating the aggression she had triggered. "Let me into the house, Nicole. We do this peaceably or you'll be facing a court order for visitation rights. You want our daughter dragged into that kind of conflict?"

She shrank back against the door, confused and frightened by the threat, not having imagined he would feel so strongly about claiming his child. But he did. The need to forge a bond with his daughter was raging through him, fuelled by the sense of having been arbitrarily deleted from being a factor in her life for the past four years. On the other hand, if he alienated Nicole too far, he wouldn't get all he wanted.

He tempered the tumult of feeling, forcing himself to speak calmly. "Let's move on from the past, Nicole. We have a future to build for Zoe and cooperation is a better foundation than conflict. Okay?"

Her hand fluttered to her throat as though it was too constricted to allow speech. Her eyes filled with a helpless vulnerability, as though he'd stripped her of defences and she didn't know which way to turn.

"It will be okay. I promise you," Quin pressed earnestly.

She scooped in a deep breath, released it in a shuddering sigh, then stepped back, pushing the door wide open to let him enter. "That's the first really important promise you've made to me, Quin," she said shakily. "I hope it will be kept."

He stopped beside her, lifting a hand to gently cup her face and tilt it towards his, wanting her to look and see the burning sincerity in his eyes. "Let's seal it with a kiss, Nicole."

He didn't wait for a verbal consent. It was enough that she kept looking at him, making no attempt to twist out of his light grasp. The need to connect with her, as well as their daughter, surged through Quin, dictating a kiss of persuasion, not possession. It was important to soothe her concerns, make her feel that he truly, deeply, cared, and the strong sexual desire she'd always stirred in him was not the one and only reason for them to come together.

For a few moments she was completely passive, letting him kiss her but not engaging in it herself. Then her inner tension collapsed and her lips moved in a tentative response, as though curious to taste what he was offering, unsure where he was going with it. Quin didn't push for more. Gaining acceptance and making it stick had to be his primary goal this morning.

He withdrew slowly, softly brushing his

lips against hers as he murmured, "A new beginning. For the three of us."

"You'd better make the most of this time with Zoe," she said huskily. "You know the way to her bedroom."

It was a dismissal but not a hostile one.

Satisfied that he had made some breakthrough, albeit a small one, Quin moved on down the hall and quietly opened the door to their daughter's bedroom, quite happy just to look at her if she was still asleep.

He hated having missed four years of her life, deprived of seeing her grow into the child she was now. He should have been familiar with her face and every expression of it. As it was, he was acutely conscious of the need to memorise it so he could call it to mind whenever he wanted.

Zoe was not asleep. She was lying on her side, gazing at the butterfly tree. Early morning sunshine was pouring through the bay window, lighting up the multicoloured wings, creating a magical sight. A child's wonderland, he thought, giving him a quick appreciation of how loving a mother Nicole had to be. How many women would put their time into such a project?

Then Zoe caught sight of him and scrambled to sit up, a look of pure amazement breaking into a smile of absolute delight. "You came again!"

The tension he had carried into this room instantly slipped away. Deep pleasure in the artless welcome from his daughter warmed his own smile. "And I brought you a present."

He handed her the boutique bag and sat on the bed beside her, happy to watch her surprise, her eager anticipation as she removed the tissue-wrapped glass butterfly, her look of awe when the gift was revealed.

"A Ulysses!" she cried. "How did you know I wanted this one, Daddy?"

"I didn't know." He was amazed she knew the name of the butterfly. "I just noticed last night that you didn't have one on your tree."

"I saw them on TV and I asked Mummy could I have one and she said I had to wait for a special occasion."

"Well, this is a very special occasion," Quin assured her.

"Yes, it is!" Zoe clapped her hands with glee. "My first day with my daddy!"

Something curled around Quin's heart and squeezed it tight.

How many first days had there been?

The day she was born…he didn't even know her birthday!

Her first word…

Her first step…

"Do all the butterflies on your tree mark special occasions, Zoe?" he asked, working hard at keeping his tone light and interested, belying the clawing sense of loss at having been eliminated from every significant signpost in her life.

"Mmm…" She cocked her head, considering her answer. "Most of them I got when I was sick. That was when Mummy started the tree."

Quin frowned over this information. "Were you very sick?"

"Very, very, very sick," she replied, nodding gravely. "I had to be in the hospital 'cause I got…" She hesitated, frowning over the name given to her malady. "Mingitis," came the triumphant recollection.

A chill ran down Quin's spine. "Do you mean…meningitis, Zoe?"

"Yes. That's it!" She looked pleased with his knowledge and repeated the word with careful precision. "Men-in-gitis."

Horror struck hard. Zoe could have died. It was probably a miracle she had survived the deadly illness. He might never have known this beautiful child had ever existed. *His* child...lost before he had found her.

"I'm sorry I wasn't there to make you feel better," he said, heaving a sigh to ease the ache in his chest.

"You were in your other world?"

"Yes." He was intensely grateful for her simple acceptance of what he'd said last night. "I didn't know what was happening to you. I wish I had known."

"That's all right, Daddy. You couldn't help it."

He would certainly help it from now on, Quin fiercely resolved.

"I was too sick to get out of bed when I was in the hospital," Zoe went on. "Mummy said I was like a little caterpillar in a cocoon and I had to wait there until I was strong enough to be a butterfly, free to dance in the open air and feel beautiful."

"You *are* beautiful."

Her eyes shone with happiness. He wanted to pick her up and hug her tight but caution insisted not yet. It might be too soon for her to feel comfortable with it. He was still virtually a stranger to her, despite their blood relationship.

"Let's find a place for the Ulysses on the tree," she cried excitedly, throwing off the bed-covers and jumping onto the floor. With the glass butterfly being carefully carried in her little hands, she was halfway to the bay window when she stopped, glancing back at him.

Quin hadn't moved. He was entranced by everything about his daughter; the cute girly way she walked, the soft roundness of her arms and legs, the smooth perfection of her young skin, the black bob of thick hair somewhat awry from a night in bed.

He was smiling and she flashed him a quick smile in response before saying, "I've got to get Mummy. She sticks the butterflies on the tree with glue tac."

"Right!" he approved.

"And I have to go to the bathroom," she confessed shyly.

"We all need to do that when we first get up in the morning," he assured her.

Relieved by his understanding, she rushed back and handed him her gift. "You mind the Ulysses until I come back." Her big grey eyes flashed an eloquent appeal. "Don't go away."

"I'll stay right here."

"That's good, Daddy."

Another quick smile and she was off, pelting out of the bedroom to do what had to be done in double-quick time.

He heard her calling out to Mummy and Nanna, her high childish voice bubbling with excitement. Quin had to concede that both women had given his daughter a loving home and brought her up to be a wonderfully natural child. Even the trauma of a serious illness had not left a shadow on her life.

He probably hadn't been missed at all.

Nobody missed what they hadn't ever known.

Nicole was worried about his intrusion, worried about its effect on Zoe. She didn't trust him to follow through on this initial impact. Quin realised that only time would prove her wrong, but how long was it going to take? He had already lost too much time he could never get back.

He looked down at the blue butterfly Zoe had placed in his hands as a surety against his departing before she returned. At least his daughter trusted in his word. Quin vowed she'd never have reason not to trust it. While it might be impossible to shield her from pain in her life, he would try his utmost not to be the cause of it.

And one thing Nicole could not deny—he had given his daughter pleasure this morning. Every opportunity he had, he would continue to do so. What he needed to do was set up as many opportunities as possible.

Zoe came racing back into the room, Nicole following her reluctantly despite the excited urging. "Come and see, Mummy. It's made of glass. Show her, Daddy."

Nicole flashed him a hard, resentful look.

Quin stood up, holding out the gift to his daughter. "You show her, Zoe. It's yours."

She took it carefully and turned to her mother who hadn't wanted him to buy it, who'd refused to take it from him. He now understood Nicole's intensely negative attitude towards it. Butterflies were too intimately connected to the life of her daughter—a life he hadn't shared and wasn't intended to ever share.

"I think it will be too heavy for glue tac to hold it on the tree, Zoe," she said with a seriously concerned look on her face. "You wouldn't want it to fall off and break."

Quin felt himself tensing up.

Okay, he hadn't been a part of the tree but he'd been given no choice in Nicole's decision to keep him ignorant of his daughter's existence. Given the chance, he would have been here for Zoe, looking after her as best he could. To deny him a place at this point in time was being deliberately obstructive to any new beginning. If she couldn't give this much…

"But, Mummy, we have to put it on," Zoe insisted. "It's my first butterfly from Daddy. Could we tie it to a branch?"

Out of the mouths of babes, Quin thought, looking at Nicole to see how she would fight the challenge from their daughter.

"That would spoil the look of it, Zoe. It's too beautiful to put string around it. Why don't we just put it on the windowsill and pretend it's fluttered down to rest there?"

Zoe swung around to face the bay window and study the position. After a few moments she walked over and carefully placed the Ulysses on the sill, then stood back to gauge the effect. She slowly shook her head. "It's not the same as being on the tree, Mummy. It looks lonely down there."

The outcast, Quin thought grimly.

"Well, maybe your father will buy more in the future to keep it company," Nicole answered, her eyes glittering a fierce challenge at him.

"This won't be a one time thing, Zoe," he quickly assured her, also notifying Nicole he was not about to go missing in the future. "But if you want the Ulysses on the tree, I'll buy a silver chain to tie it on and make it shine even more beautifully. How about that?"

Her little face lit up with delight. "Oh, that would make it very special, Daddy!"

"Right!" He didn't care how much Nicole might resent it. In fact, seizing opportunity rather than waiting for it seemed a very good idea. "I'll bring the chain with me on Saturday morning and if it's okay with your mother, we could spend the whole day together."

"Mummy?" Zoe cried expectantly.

Nicole forced a smile for her daughter. "Okay. Now I think you should get dressed and go and have the breakfast Nanna is preparing for you."

"Can Daddy have breakfast with me?" she asked eagerly.

"No, your father has to go to work. That's why he's wearing a suit. It was very good of him to come this morning especially to see you. Have you thanked him for his gift?"

"Oh, no, I haven't!" Zoe looked at him, appalled at having forgotten to do so.

Seizing opportunity again, Quin smiled encouragingly and held out his arms to her. "How about a hug and a kiss?"

She flew at him in happy relief. Quin lifted her up against his shoulder and her little arms wound around his neck as she planted a big wet kiss on his cheek. "Thank you, Daddy. I love my Ulysses."

It was said with such fervour, Quin felt his heart turn over. It was all he could do to control his embrace and not squeeze her too tightly. This beautiful child was his and he didn't want to let her out of his possession. Then he caught sight of the pained look in Nicole's eyes and knew that pushing this visit any further would be counter-productive to holding the ground he'd already taken.

"I'm glad it's very special for you, Zoe," he murmured, his voice husky with pleasure. "I'll come again on Saturday."

"Don't get lost in your other world again, will you, Daddy?"

"No. Now that I've found you, there's no chance of that happening."

"Good!"

She grinned happily at him and he grinned right back as he set her down on her feet. "Better do what Mummy says. Bye for now, Zoe."

"You won't forget the silver chain?"

"I'll go shopping for it at lunchtime today. You work out where you'd like to hang the Ulysses on the tree, and we'll do it first thing on Saturday morning."

She sighed her contentment.

"Be a good girl for Mummy," he said in parting.

"I will. Bye, Daddy."

Nicole accompanied him out of the bedroom in tight-lipped silence, shutting the door behind them. As they walked down the hall, Quin asked, "Do you have any photo albums of Zoe's life so far?"

"Yes," came the curt, uninviting answer.

"I'd like to see them," he pressed.

"I'll bring them with me on Friday night."

Not letting them out of her possession.

"Thank you. And thank you for Zoe, too, Nicole. She's a wonderful child."

"Yes, she is."

It was said so vehemently, he could hear the unspoken words—*And you'd better not change that, Quin Sola!*

They stepped out on the front porch and Nicole halted by the front door. "Don't start spoiling her with what your money can buy, Quin," she warned.

He nodded. Money was the big issue between them. Quin realised they could not truly make a new beginning until he'd addressed Nicole's perception of him.

"We'll have a lot to talk about on Friday night," he said, locking eyes with her. "Whatever you feel I did or didn't do in the time we lived together, you've paid me back with a vengeance, Nicole, withholding my child from me all these years."

She flinched at the hit, then lifted her chin defiantly. "It was for the best."

"We'll never know, will we? Just don't forget the photo albums. That would be inflicting serious injury on top of insult."

He left her with those words.

There was a lot to be organised and achieved before Friday night.

CHAPTER TWELVE

NICOLE had not heard from Quin since Tuesday morning, not by telephone nor by e-mail. She arrived at his apartment at eight o'clock on Friday evening, not knowing what to expect from him, trying not to expect anything but the usual sex-fest that charac-terised their nights together.

This was the thirteenth night, and while she wasn't superstitious, Nicole could not shake an ominous feeling about it. The deal was still on but the limits of the situation had changed with Quin's knowledge of Zoe and his determination to be a father to their daughter.

A new beginning…but a new beginning to what?

Was Quin capable of making the future different to the past?

She was carrying a much larger bag than

usual, having brought the photo albums he'd requested and her grip on its handles was so tight, her nails were digging into her palm as she waited for the door to open. It hurt to let Quin into the years that had belonged to her and Zoe. She felt she was giving up too much too soon. If he didn't keep his promise…

The door opened.

Her heart skittered nervously as she came face-to-face with Quin again. He beamed her a welcoming smile which she couldn't return. The turbulence in her mind and stomach overrode any normal civility.

"Come on in," he said warmly. "There's someone here I want you to meet."

Shock completely paralysed any movement forward. She couldn't believe he would bring a third party into a night of personal and private revelations. Or weren't the photos of Zoe's life important to him— just a curiosity which could be satisfied any time at all?

Her mouth finally returned to working order. Enough to say, "I don't think so, Quin." Glaring steely determination, she added, "Our deal doesn't involve anyone else."

He sucked in a deep breath. The bullet-grey eyes seared hers with their own determination and the welcoming air changed to ruthless purpose. "It's my mother, Nicole. Come all the way from Argentina to meet you and her grand-daughter."

His mother!

Whom she had never been invited to meet in the past!

Nicole's mind reeled over this totally unexpected move from Quin. What did he mean to gain by it? How was she supposed to respond?

"Argentina?" she repeated dazedly.

"That's where her family lives. My mother returned there three years ago to be with them. It's her home country."

"Yours, too?" Nicole croaked, desperately trying to slot this new information into her very limited knowledge of Quin's background.

A careless shrug accompanied his reply. "Not anymore. I've made my home here. Please…my mother is tired from the fourteen-hour flight from Buenos Aires, but she wants so much to meet you…"

He stepped back, beckoning Nicole into his penthouse. Her feet moved, pulled by a curiosity that demanded satisfaction. As Quin ushered her past the open kitchen area, she saw a woman rising to her feet from one of the leather sofas near the view of the harbour—a tall, handsome woman, whose strong-boned face was etched with fatigue, her heavy-lidded, dark eyes looking almost bruised by the shadows around them.

Her only make-up appeared to be a plum-red lipstick, and her iron-grey hair was pulled back into a neat bun. Despite this austerity, or because of it, she exuded a rather intimidating dignity, probably enhanced by the stylish black suit she wore and the jet earrings and necklace, all of which made Nicole feel overwhelmingly underdressed for this meeting in her jeans and peasant blouse.

Her feet faltered, coming to a halt as the thought struck that she was probably viewed as a loose woman by Quin's mother—living with her son, having his child out of wedlock, not even telling him about the pregnancy so they couldn't be properly married as *good girls* undoubtedly would in Argentina. A tide of hot embarrassment raced up her neck and burnt her cheeks even as she feverishly reasoned this was all Quin's fault, not hers. She'd done what *he'd* wanted until it had become too…too *wrong!*

Quin pried the carry-bag from her grip, passing it to his other hand as he took hold of her elbow to draw her forward. "Nicole, this is my mother, Evita Gallardo."

"Not…not Sola?" Nicole babbled in bewilderment.

"When I returned home, I resumed my maiden name," Quin's mother explained, wincing apologetically at her son as she added, "There was too much shame attached to the name of Sola."

"Shame?" Nicole repeated, feeling utterly confused.

Quin's mother had moved to meet her and was now holding out both hands in what seemed like appeal…or was it in greeting? Nicole quickly offered her own and they were taken and pressed, the dark eyes of Evita Gallardo suddenly transmitting an anxious concern.

"It is a long story," she said. "And I have come because I owe it to you. I hope you will understand."

Understand what? Nicole almost blurted out, but conscious of already sounding like a parrot, she constrained herself to nodding. Then realising she hadn't even greeted the woman, she hastily said, "I'm very pleased to meet you, Mrs.…um… Miss…? Gallardo."

"Please…call me Evita. We are already family. You have borne me a grand-daughter," came the soft reasoning.

"Right," Nicole agreed, relieved to see no hint of criticism in the dark eyes. There seemed to be more a wish—a need?—for acceptance.

Because of Zoe!

The answer was so obvious, Nicole berated herself for getting uptight about her own impact on Quin's mother. Regardless of how she was viewed, Evita Gallardo would undoubtedly be very guarded against offending the legal custodian of her grandchild. This meeting had to be about establishing amenable contact, opening a gateway into Zoe's life. Which meant Quin had to be very seriously intent on being a constant part of their daughter's future.

"I brought some albums with photos of Zoe," she said, impulsively offering to Evita Gallardo what she had begrudged giving to Quin. Somehow it was different—woman to woman with the shared knowledge of how it was to have a child. "Perhaps you would like to look through them."

"I would like it very much." She squeezed Nicole's hands in fervent gratitude, then released one to wave her own towards the sofa she'd left. "Please come and sit with me."

"Coffee, Nicole?" Quin asked, distracting her momentarily from his mother.

His eyes glimmered with satisfaction, giving Nicole the instant impression this scenario was going exactly as he had planned. Ruthless in going after what he wanted, she thought, but what end did he have in mind? He'd caught her by surprise with this introduction to his mother, and Nicole could feel any control over what would happen next slipping right out of her hands. She saw no alternative but to ride this evening through as best she could. "Yes, please," she answered.

At least having coffee when she first arrived was normal routine. After their first night together she had declined any further dinner invitations, preferring to eat the evening meal with her mother and Zoe before she left home. Besides which, dining out with Quin had seemed too much like dating and she'd wanted to keep the deal a deal with a finish line, not slide back into a relationship with him.

As she accompanied his mother to the sofa, Nicole reflected that it was now impossible to avoid an ongoing relationship, given Quin's stated commitment to being far more than a nominal father to Zoe. Involving his mother was definite proof of how serious he was about it.

Though his mother would undoubtedly return to her home in Argentina and visits from her would probably be few and far between, so her presence here tonight didn't really prove anything.

Nicole sternly cautioned herself against taking mental leaps into a future that might not materialise. She sat down with Evita Gallardo, very conscious that she should take only one step at a time in this murky situation. Assume nothing. Trust nothing. Just go with the flow tonight.

Quin placed her carry-bag on the coffee table in front of them. "Wait for me before you start with the albums," he said. "I don't want to miss anything."

His eyes seared hers with the message he'd missed far too much already and Nicole inwardly bridled at the implied accusation of having shut him out from where he should have been. If he'd given *her* any sense of commitment during their two-year relationship, she wouldn't have chosen to be a single parent.

"Of course, we will wait," his mother answered a touch anxiously, as though pleasing her son was of paramount importance.

Quin headed off to the kitchen to make coffee and Nicole turned to Evita Gallardo, wanting the background information that Quin had always denied her. "You said the name of Sola carried too much shame. Would you explain that to me, Evita?"

She sighed heavily, giving Nicole the distinct impression that it took a huge effort to reveal a history, which was obviously a source of personal pain and embarrassment. The dark eyes held sadness and deep regrets as she began to speak.

"My husband, Luis Sola, was a very handsome, very charming, very clever man. I was...under his spell...for many years, believing he was everything he portrayed himself to be. But he used our marriage to gain access to people of wealth he would not have met otherwise, and he defrauded them, as well as members of my family, of a great deal of money. One day, everything seemed normal, and the next he was gone, leaving me and our son to face the scandal of his treachery."

"That must have been very difficult," Nicole murmured sympathetically.

Evita shook her head and heaved another sigh. "I could not bear it. And it was particularly bad for Joaquin, who had to carry the stigma of his father's crimes at school. He was only thirteen and suddenly he was ostracised from everything. Even my family shunned him. Because he looked so very much like Luis, he was most unfairly cast as a bad seed who would also bring shame upon us all."

"But you didn't believe that," Nicole said encouragingly, caught up in the story and wanting to hear more.

"I know my son. He is a Gallardo through and through." There was a flash of pride in the pained eyes. "It was better for him that we accept exile in Australia than to stay in Buenos Aires where he would never be trusted. So we came here and Joaquin vowed he would prove them all wrong."

"How?"

"By making restitution, returning all the stolen money."

This was the driving force behind his single-minded ambition to make as much money as he could, Nicole realised, stunned by how little she had known about the man she had loved.

"Once we were settled here, he worked very hard. Studied hard," his mother went on. "He won a special scholarship to a university and got a business degree, then moved straight into a bank to learn how to make money from money."

"Which he proceeded to do with extraordinary success. The star player," Nicole commented wryly.

Evita nodded, then eyed her ruefully. "When he met you and left the house my father had provided for us to be with you, it meant his feeling for you was very strong. It worried me that it would pull him away from fulfilling what I had dreamt about—returning to Buenos Aires with great pride in my son and what he had achieved."

She lifted her hands in an appeal for forgiveness as she added, "I would not meet you. I would not give you any status in Joaquin's life. I would not let him even speak of you to me. So it is because of my selfishness…"

"You don't have to go that far, *Madre*,"

Quin interrupted as he carried the cappuccino over to where they sat. "I wasn't about
to let anything prevent me from achieving
what I'd resolved to do." He set the coffee
cup down on the table and looked straight at
Nicole. "I thought I could have my cake and
eat it, too, but in doing so, I lost far more than
I'd bargained for."

Zoe, he meant.

The restitution mission had won out over
any commitment to the relationship they'd
shared, no matter how strongly he had felt
about her. Though she guessed the deep-
seated trauma of what had happened when
he was thirteen was not something that could
be easily set aside, especially when he had
the end-goal in his sights.

"I presume you did win respectability
back in Buenos Aires since your mother now
lives there," she remarked.

"Yes. All the debts were paid with interest
three years ago," he answered almost cynically, no pride at all in his achievement.

His mother promptly supplied the pride.
"It was such an honourable deed, my family
finally embraced him as one of their own."

"Why didn't you stay?" Nicole asked,

curious to know why he'd turned his back on the status of hero.

His eyes flashed mockingly. "My name is Joaquin Luis Sola. I am still my father's son, and that means nothing in Australia."

"A clean slate," Nicole interpreted.

"Not so clean." His gaze dropped to the carry-bag. "Could we look at the photo albums now?"

His mother's words—*an honourable deed*—kept playing through Nicole's mind as she removed the albums from the bag and stacked them on the table in the right order. Was his *not so clean slate* centred on Zoe now? Was it a matter of honour for him to be a good father to his daughter?

Honour wasn't love.

And neither was lust.

She would have to be very, very careful not to colour Quin's current moves with feelings he didn't have. That could lead to big mistakes, and it wasn't just herself who would end up paying for them. She didn't want Zoe's innocent acceptance of Quin as her father to result in a long string of hurtful disappointments. Though how she could prevent that now, she didn't know.

He sat down beside her as she rested the

oldest album on her lap, ready to turn to the first baby photograph of Zoe. It meant she was sandwiched between her daughter's father and grandmother on the long leather sofa, and the sense of inevitable involvement with both of them weighed heavily on her mind and heart, making her feel tremulous inside.

She couldn't stop her hand from shaking a little as she opened the album and her voice turned husky from a sudden welling of emotion. "This is Zoe on the day she was born."

She looked so tiny in the hospital baby trolley, all bundled up with only her face showing—a rather red face framed by a surprisingly thick mass of spiky black hair. Her eyes were shut and the crescents of long thick eyelashes were also stunningly black.

"Oh! She looks just like Joaquin when he was born!" Evita marvelled, clasping her hands over her heart as though all her prayers had been answered.

"No, *Madre*." Quin's arm reached out, a finger gently touching the baby's full lower lip in the photograph. "This perfectly shaped mouth comes directly from Nicole. And Zoe is very much a little girl, not a boy."

A mouth he knew all too intimately, Nicole thought, feeling his strongly muscled thigh pressing against hers and cravenly wishing there was more than hot sex driving the desire that constantly simmered between them. It hurt that there wasn't, even more now than it had in the past as she continued to show the baby photographs of their daughter whom she now had to share with him.

After that first correction to his mother, he sat in silence, intently viewing the progression of Zoe's infancy to the toddler stage. It was Evita who peppered Nicole with questions and made increasingly infatuated comments about her beautiful grand-daughter. Quin just looked, and Nicole grew more and more conscious of tension emanating him, a turbulent tension that swirled with all he restrained himself from saying. She could feel him thinking, *I missed out on this, and this, and this*...and the bitter vengefulness that had driven many of her thoughts and actions started sliding into guilt.

Had she been terribly wrong to keep Zoe from him?

His silence continued through the second album and almost to end of the third. It wasn't until Nicole turned a page to reveal a much thinner Zoe standing beside the newly constructed butterfly tree, that he made a sound—a low gravelly rumble in his throat. Then...

"This must be after she was struck down with meningitis."

"Meningitis!" Evita cried in horror.

Shock rolled through Nicole. She had not told Quin of Zoe's illness so how did he know? Her head jerked around to look at him and she caught a poignant look of pain and anger in his eyes before he bent forward to answer his mother.

"Fortunately Zoe recovered with no long-term ill effects from it, *Madre*. And Nicole came up with the brilliant idea of creating a butterfly tree to help her look forward to being completely well again. Which she is. Delightfully so," he added gruffly.

Zoe must have told him when he gave her the Ulysses butterfly. He was glossing over the terrible worry of that time to soothe his mother's concerns, but Nicole was deeply disturbed by the reaction he was now covering up. Did he really care so much? Had she been selfishly unfair in depriving him of his child?

As she proceeded to leaf through the fourth and last album where the photographs demonstrated beyond doubt that their daughter was, indeed, a normal healthy little girl, her mind kept zipping to the fact that Quin would have been free of the long hangover from his father's crimes when Zoe contracted meningitis. But even after he'd returned from Argentina, he had obviously continued to pursue the accumulation of wealth, so he wouldn't have had much time to give to a sick child, anyway.

It was all very well for him to think he might have acted differently. Nicole told herself he had a lot to prove before she'd be convinced his priorities had been reshuffled. Though he had walked away from a business client so as not to lose his time with her. Then visiting Zoe on Tuesday morning…

"Oh! She's learning ballet!" Evita exclaimed in delight.

It was the last photograph in the album—Zoe in her pink dancing costume with a many layered tulle tutu, striking a typical pose with arms arched above her head, one foot planted firmly on the floor and the other pointed.

"She's into all forms of dance," Nicole answered. "My mother has a dance school and I teach there. Zoe has been attending children's classes most of her life. Not because I put her into them. She just loves dancing."

"Do you think she would dance for me while I'm here?" Evita asked hopefully.

"Let's not leap too far ahead, *Madre*," Quin swiftly interposed as Nicole closed the album, her mind whirling around his mother's request and not finding a ready reply.

It seemed stupid to feel fearful, yet she had only met Evita Gallardo tonight and she'd had no time to think about introducing another grandmother to Zoe. The sense of being trapped into acknowledging a relationship instead of having a choice about it raised a wave of panic. First, Quin. Now his mother in quick succession. It seemed as though the special bond she had with her daughter was being threatened.

"I did not mean to presume," Evita said, anxiety in her voice and in the hand that reached out and pressed Nicole's. "I am very tired, and seeing the photographs…" She sighed, patting Nicole's hand reassuringly. "I will retire to my room now and leave you with Joaquin to decide on what is appropriate."

Quin stood as his mother rose from the

sofa and quickly moved to take her arm. "Is there anything you need, *Madre?*" he asked caringly.

"No." She leaned against him for a moment, then squared her shoulders and nodded to Nicole. "Good night, my dear. I am sorry our meeting was so long delayed."

Nicole returned the nod, unable to bring herself to say anything beyond a courteous, "Good night."

"Stay, Joaquin," his mother commanded. "I can make my own way to my room."

"If you're sure…"

"Yes." She kissed his cheek and walked off alone.

"I'm going to drive Nicole home now. I won't be gone long. An hour at most," he assured her.

Was that *it* for tonight?

Nicole sat in stunned disbelief, watching Quin watch his mother move to the hall leading to the bedrooms.

Then it hit her.

No sex on Monday night.

No sex tonight.

The deal had become irrelevant.

Everything now centred on Zoe.

CHAPTER THIRTEEN

NICOLE didn't notice the class or the comfort of Quin's Audi as he drove it through the city to link up with Parramatta Road which would take them directly to Burwood. She was far too acutely aware of the man sitting beside her and the burning issues that lay between them. They hadn't spoken since leaving his apartment and the silence tore at her nerves.

Having worked some moisture into her dry mouth she asked, "How long will your mother be staying?"

"Until the wedding," came the matter-of-fact reply.

She looked sharply at him. "What wedding?"

Quin flicked her a glittering glance that mocked the question. "The wedding that should have taken place five years ago," he drawled, returning his attention to the road ahead.

She gritted her teeth, barely containing a fierce wave of resentment at his assumption. When she could bring herself to speak again with some semblance of control, the words were grated out with biting emphasis. "We lived together for two years, Quin. Marriage was not on your agenda. I didn't want and still don't want a shotgun wedding because of an accidental pregnancy."

"It *was* accidental then?"

"I certainly didn't plan it," she threw at him, shocked that he could think otherwise.

"You were supposed to be taking a highly effective birth control pill," he reminded her.

"My doctor explained it can lose its effect if one has a bad stomach upset. You might recall the food poisoning I got from a party we attended," she answered curtly, then shot him a puzzled look. "Why on earth would you think I'd deliberately get pregnant?"

He shook his head. "I'm trying to understand why you didn't tell me. Zoe is part of me, too, Nicole. Why couldn't you share her with me? I've missed so much…"

"Why couldn't you share with me what your mother told me tonight?" she shot back at him, refusing to let guilt worm through her consciousness.

"It had nothing to do with you," he answered, instantly justifying the decisions she'd made five years ago.

"You're right!" she snapped. "I was only ever on the edge of your life, not at the heart of it. I couldn't live like that with you any more. And I didn't want it for Zoe, either."

"You were at the heart of pleasure for me, Nicole," he said quietly. "The other was pain."

"Well let me tell you, Quin, love is about sharing both pain and pleasure, and you'd better start learning that if you intend to be a good father to Zoe."

Her voice shook with the strong emotions that had been coursing through her all evening, and she tried valiantly to clamp down on them, not wanting to reveal how much she wanted his love, how much she had always wanted it. His focus on their daughter was actually making her feel jealous of Zoe, and that couldn't lead anywhere good.

They stopped at a red traffic light and Quin turned to her, a deadly serious expression on his face, his eyes intensely concentrated on hers, making her heart thump in the helpless hope she was important to him—deeply, irrevocably important to him. Not just for the pleasure of the sexual intimacy they could so easily achieve. Not because she was the mother of his child. She needed to be the woman he loved above all others, the one he truly would share his life with. All of it. Not some piece he selected to give, excluding her from other parts.

"What you heard from my mother tonight…it wasn't only my life story, Nicole," he said earnestly. "It was hers, too. A very private, painful story that drove her into exile from her home country. She didn't want it told to anyone here. And that wasn't ever going to end until I ended it, as I did when I paid back the money. I'm free of it now, free to take on other responsibilities and give them the attention they should have."

Responsibilities…was that how he thought of marriage and fatherhood? She didn't want it to be a point of honour for him to marry her—a responsibility he had take on and carry for the rest of his life.

"I understand you felt…sidelined…when we were together before," he went on. "I can't go back and change that, but I promise you it will be different this time."

"What? No sex?" she scoffed, the crass challenge spilling out of her own thwarted desire for him, heating her whole body with an instant wave of shame.

For several seconds the air in the car was charged with steaming frustrations—his and hers. Then a car-horn behind them honked its driver's frustration. The red traffic light had turned green. Quin switched his attention back to the road, put his foot on the accelerator and the Audi responded with a swift surge of speed.

"As much sex as you like," he growled, once they were travelling smoothly again.

Nicole couldn't stop herself from sniping, "Really? I thought that had been sidelined since you met your daughter."

"There've been other things to consider," came the terse reply.

"Like planning a wedding without bothering to get my consent?"

"Like trying to clear up the past so we can build a future on mutual trust."

"We need more than trust to build a future."

"I thought great sex was a given, but if you need that reinforced…"

"I wasn't talking about sex."

"Yes, you were." His eyes smoked anger at her. "If that's the only thing I'm good for, as far as you're concerned, I'll make it so good you can't live without it."

He deftly manoeuvred the Audi across traffic lanes as he spoke and suddenly took a left hand turn, startling Nicole into asking, "What are you doing?"

"Going to a hotel where we'll be assured of absolute privacy."

Her heart catapulted around her chest. She hadn't been talking about sex. Love had been on her mind. Trust and love. Yet she couldn't deny the adrenaline rush at the exciting thought of going to bed with Quin, having him to herself again, drowning out the confusion and conflicts of the past few days with sheer, mind-blasting physical chemistry.

Though it wouldn't solve anything, she told herself, and surrendering to this move without a protest would probably make Quin think he had the power to push her into whatever he wanted. "You told your mother you were taking me home and would soon be back," she rattled out.

It made no impact on him. He turned the car into Elizabeth Street, heading towards

Circular Quay instead of out of the city centre. "My mother has my cell-phone number," he stated reasonably. "I doubt she'll worry about where I am but she can always call me to find out."

There was no answer to that.

"And *your* mother won't be expecting you home tonight," he added, shooting her a derisive look. "Right?"

He was referring to the deal.

It was the thirteenth night—a night for which he'd paid an exorbitant amount of money and she had to deliver what had been promised. No argument. The weird part was she had wanted the deal back in place, resenting his involvement with their daughter and the intrusion of his mother, yet now that Quin was obliging her…why was she feeling so at odds with it?

Because too much else was involved now.

And as much as she wanted to, she couldn't just forget how far he seemed determined to push himself into her life.

They turned into the entrance driveway of a very grand hotel facing Hyde Park. As soon as the Audi halted, a doorman and a parking attendant offered their services. With the car taken care of, they were ushered into a palatial lobby and Quin wasted no time in securing a suite. Within a few minutes, they were in a plush elevator, zooming up to their designated floor.

"Amazing what having lots of money can accomplish," Nicole remarked cynically, thinking of the speed with which Quin's requirements had been met.

"Yes, it wiped out my mother's disgrace, your mother's debts, got you back into bed with me…"

The harshly cynical retort jerked her gaze up to his. Soul-searing anger looked back at her. It stirred all the fermenting emotions that had been plaguing her since he had found out about Zoe.

"You're trying to take more than your pound of flesh, Quin."

"I have a right to more than you agreed to give me."

"You want to be a father to our daughter…fine! But that doesn't mean I have to be your wife."

The elevator doors opened. Quin grasped her arm, steering her out of the compartment, along a corridor, halting briefly to unlock and open the door to their suite, then pulling her inside and kicking the door shut behind them. The fierce turbulence emanating from him was all too evident when he swung her into his embrace for a close face to face confrontation. Stormy-grey eyes raged at her brittle defences.

"Why not? Why not be my wife? You want this as much as I do."

His mouth crashed down on hers, igniting all the pent-up lust that should have been simple and straightforward and easily satisfied with Quin making himself sexually available for this thirteenth night. Nicole responded to his savage plundering with a passionate abandonment of every other concern, but she could not stop her heart yearning for more than a physical union.

Her arms wound around his neck, holding him with a wanton possessiveness. Her body plastered itself to his, seeking its heat, its strength, wanting its rampant need to envelop her, seep into her, fill her with the sense that only she could be his life mate. Her breasts were crushed against his chest, her stomach furrowed by the hard roll of his erection, her thighs quivering under the muscular power pressing against them. A wild chant was running through her mind— *love me, love me, love me…*

He rained kisses on her face, her hair, her neck, her shoulders, and she gloried in the feeling that his mouth was branding her as his. His hands slid down and clutched her bottom, pressing her closer and she ground herself against him in a delirium of desire. He lifted her off her feet, keeping her pinned to him as he strode across the room. They landed on a bed, his body covering hers, their hands tearing at each other's clothes in a frenzied need to be rid of all barriers between them.

At last they were naked, panting from the wild haste to come together. Quin took her hands and slammed them above her head, assuming a domination she would not allow him to have. As he hovered over her, his face close to hers, his eyes blazing an arrogantly male ownership, she lifted her legs and locked them around his hips, her own eyes hotly defying him to deny the possession was mutual.

"Tell me it's never been like this with anyone else," he demanded, his voice a harsh rasp, as though scraped from feelings he didn't want to acknowledge, but they were bursting through him and couldn't be contained.

"You tell me the same thing," she fiercely challenged.

"There's been no other woman in my life who could match you in any respect," he conceded.

"Well, you top the list, too," she retorted, jealously wondering how many women that amounted to. "So far," she added to stop him thinking he had it made with her and nothing more was required of him in the longer term.

"Are you expecting to do better?" he growled.

"Maybe the best is yet to come," she answered, goading him to take their relationship to deeper levels.

"You're right," he said unexpectedly, a wolfish grin breaking out on his darkly handsome face. "We haven't got there yet. Just let me get a condom out ready."

"You don't have to use one tonight."

"Then the best—" his lips brushed over hers in tantalisingly seductive play as he murmured "—can certainly be achieved."

And he kissed her so erotically, her mind spun with sensual excitement and every nerve in her body zinged with anticipation of the intense pleasure Quin would undoubtedly deliver. Which he did. Pure physical bliss. Her entire being hummed with delicious exultation as he drove her through climax after climax. Somehow it was like an ecstatic celebration of being a woman, feeling every part of her femininity being loved, adored, savoured, and she revelled in every moment of it.

And she knew in her heart of hearts, that she would only ever respond to Quin like this. She didn't understand why it was so, but in some deeply primitive way she belonged with him. Maybe it was wrong to expect him to think and feel as she did. He was a man with a strong hunter's instinct, a man who would always go after what he wanted, letting nothing distract him from his prime target.

Could she blame him for being what he was?

Hadn't that always been an integral part of his attraction?

She let herself love him with her hands, her mouth, her legs—a sweet voluptuous loving as she moved in rhythm to the swift, concentrated drive towards his own climax, luxuriating in the fine tension of his body, knowing he was totally focused on reaching this final intimate union with her and nothing else mattered but the moment of spilling himself inside her, the hot fusion that made them one.

She lifted her body in an arch of uninhibited giving as his release came, her inner muscles convulsing in pleasure around him, and her arms tightened their embrace as he collapsed on top of her, hugging the sweet intimacy for as long as she could. Good, better, best...they were meaningless words. It was heaven being with Quin like this. Always had been.

He rolled onto his back, carrying her with him so they still lay entangled. She loved lying on top of him, feeling the rise and fall of his chest as his breathing gradually slowed to normal. He played with the long tresses of her hair, stroked her back, every caress delightfully sensual, and she couldn't imagine ever wanting to make love with anyone else.

But sex was only one part of marriage.

It hadn't been enough to keep her happy with Quin in the past. Would he really share more of himself with her this time around?

The memory of something her friend, Jade Zilic, had said on that fateful night at the Havana Club slid into her mind. It was in answer to her own comment about her previous relationship with Quin—*I don't live at that address anymore.*

Maybe he doesn't, either, Jade had remarked, going on to say that time and timing were very tricky things…shifting sands, different circumstances, revolving doors.

What had driven Quin back then was over, no longer holding any power to influence his behaviour or decisions. Maybe he could really focus on being a decent husband and father. In which case, shouldn't marriage with him be given a chance? The sands had shifted. And Quin had opened the door to fatherhood and walked right in, committing himself to being Zoe's daddy in a very real sense.

The big question was…how far could she trust his commitment?

"Did you buy the silver chain for the Ulysses butterfly?" she asked, testing if he'd remembered his promise to Zoe.

The fingers feathering down her spine stopped their caress and pressed into her skin. "Yes, I did," he answered emphatically. "I'll bring it with me tomorrow."

So he wasn't about to disappoint their daughter.

But that didn't necessarily mean he would

keep the promises made at a wedding ceremony. Zoe was his flesh and blood. Nicole wasn't. And Quin had never said he loved her.

The fingers dug in. "What about my mother, Nicole? She would love to meet Zoe."

She sighed and he lightened his touch, not pressuring for a quick reply. It wasn't easy to decide what to do about his mother. Everything felt so rushed. Yet the woman had flown all the way from Argentina to make amends for her rejection in the past. Though that might only have been because she wanted access to her grand-daughter.

Flesh and blood again.

But to get to it, Nicole Ashton could not be ignored any more. Zoe was her flesh and blood, too.

So it came down to sharing a child who not only belonged to herself and her own mother, but to Quin and his mother, too. *Everything* between herself and Quin came down to sharing and not sharing, she thought with bitter irony.

It had to be conceded that he had taken forceful steps this week to redress their previous situation, and tonight's revelations did explain a lot. They didn't make her feel any better but at least she could understand where he'd been coming from, which made acceptance of his presence in her life a little easier. And if she accepted him, she probably had to accept his mother, too.

Having come to a decision, she took a deep breath and cautiously lowered her hard-held barriers. "Not tomorrow, Quin. Zoe is expecting to have the day with you. I'll need to speak to my mother about it but perhaps we could all have lunch together on Sunday."

His tense stillness was instantly broken. An audible intake of air expanded his chest, then whooshed out as he heaved himself up and rolled Nicole onto her back. Propped on his elbow, he grinned down at her, pleasure and triumph sparkling in his eyes.

"Don't think that means we're going to talk about a wedding," she shot at him, refusing to be manoeuvred all his way.

His grin diminished into a wry little smile. "Thank you, Nicole. To my mind, there has been more than enough punishment for crimes committed. I'm glad you agree."

Punishment…she frowned over the term. Had she been punishing Quin for not loving her by keeping any knowledge of his child from him? Not consciously, though she certainly had to admit to many vengeful thoughts since meeting him again at the Havana Club.

He lifted a hand and gently smoothed the creases from her forehead. "Don't worry," he murmured in his rich velvet voice. "It will be all right. I promise you."

It was an impossible promise, Nicole thought, but she didn't want to think any more because Quin was kissing her again and stressing over the future could wait until tomorrow. Nothing was going to change between now and then.

He made it easy to pretend there was caring in his kisses, tenderness in the sensuality of his caresses. Maybe if she pretended enough, she could bring herself to believe he loved her.

And it wasn't just great sex.

CHAPTER FOURTEEN

THIS was his woman, Quin thought, holding Nicole close and revelling in the pleasure of their naked intimacy. It seemed absurd to him that she wouldn't simply accept that he was her man. The sex wouldn't be so good— so great—if they weren't in tune, instinctively meeting each other's needs, responding to whatever was wanted. Why was she resisting the idea of marrying him?

Surely she understood that nothing now stood in his way of giving a firm commitment to a future together. It would be best for Zoe to have her parents married and all three of them living under the same roof. Travelling back and forth for visits was an inefficient use of time.

Quin told himself to curb his impatience. Nicole was a very intelligent person. And reasonable. She was allowing his mother to meet Zoe. That was a big step, given that she had been shut out of his mother's life in the past. It was probably enough at this point to have planted the seed of a wedding, start her thinking about it, not push too hard. The sense of so much time lost was eating at him, but maybe his best play now was a waiting game, gradually wearing down Nicole's resistance to his plan.

She heaved a sigh, the warm spread of her breath across his chest making his skin tingle. His hand automatically began gliding down her spine, seeking more sensory pleasure. He loved every feminine curve of her body, loved the voluptuous softness of her bottom.

"You should go back to your mother, Quin. It must be hours since we left her. The hotel can call a taxi to take me home."

Unwelcome words.

He wanted to immerse himself in feeling.

"It's our night together," he said.

She hitched herself up to address him face to face. "*You* brought your mother into it. People are usually out of kilter with their sleep patterns after a long flight. If she's restless…"

"She can look after herself, Nicole."

Her expression of concern hardened to glittering mockery. "What? She's served your purpose so you don't have to give her any more attention? Still working on that basis, Quin?"

He frowned at the harsh criticism. "My mother understands how important you are to me. She understands I'll be spending as much time with you as I can."

"Of course." Her tone was bitterly ironic. "Your needs come first. They always have."

Before he could counteract the allegation she rolled away from him, off the bed and onto her feet, defiantly declaring, "I'm getting dressed and going home."

"We have a deal," he reminded her, more in frustration than with the intent of keeping her to it.

She had already bent to pick up her clothes from the floor. Very slowly she straightened up, standing with her chin lifted high, meeting his gaze with a look of fierce scorn. "How remiss of me! What with your visit to my daughter tomorrow, and your mother's visit to come on Sunday, I quite forgot I was your paid whore. Perhaps we should revise the arrangements for these family visits."

"No!"

Her arms folded belligerently. "You expect to get everything your own way, Quin?"

He'd struck the wrong note with her and the danger of losing the ground he'd made forced him into a fast re-appraisal of the situation. He propped himself on his side and grimaced apologetically, gesturing an appeal for a stay of judgement as he conceded, "Okay, I guess I'm being selfish, not wanting to let you go. The truth is… I never will have enough of you Nicole, so I'm greedy for whatever you'll give me."

"You're getting more of my time than we bargained for," she stated tersely, not softening one bit.

"I know. And I'm grateful for your generosity."

She looked away from him, thinking her own private thoughts. The tension emanating from her put Quin on edge. Should he get up and hold her, cut the distance she was putting between them? Or give her room to move whatever way *she* wanted?

He waited.

She shook her head, chiding herself as she muttered, "I agreed to stay the night. Twenty-six nights." Her gaze met his derisively. "This is the thirteenth. You still have another thirteen, Quin. I shouldn't have let myself get distracted by other considerations."

The number, thirteen, had never sounded so ominous to him. He had to change what she was trying to put back into place right now. It was suddenly very clear that not even great sex would get him what he wanted with Nicole. He quickly rose from the bed and gently grasped her upper arms to hold her still and concentrate her attention on what he had to say. Her eyes locked onto his, challenging the kind of man he was. He spoke quietly, injecting each word with intensely serious purpose.

"I don't want you as my whore, Nicole. I want you as my wife."

Instant recoil in her expression. No pause to consider. "I guess that would be very convenient for you, Quin, but I don't feel like serving your convenience for the rest of my life," she stated flatly, then nailed her point of view by adding, "I'd like you to see things my way, too."

Red Alert signals went off in Quin's brain. He instantly moved into damage control.

"You're right. We'll get dressed and go. Which I hope will prove I do care about how you feel." He tried an appealing smile. "Give me time, Nicole. I've been so fixated on forcing my way back into your life, fighting for every minute I get with you, I haven't had the chance yet to show we could have a good future together."

She searched his eyes as though she wanted to believe him but couldn't quite bring herself to do so. "You were free to come looking for me after you finished your business in Argentina three years ago. It took an accidental meeting for you to decide you wanted me again."

"I thought I'd lost you. Seeing you again made me determined to change that."

"I don't want how it was before," she cried.

"It won't be. I swear to you it won't be."

She looked uncertain, fearful.

"Give me time, Nicole," he pressed.

Her eyes closed, as though she couldn't bear to look at him any more. "Well, tomorrow is another day," she said on a deep sigh. "Let's get going."

Knowing he would win nothing by holding onto her any longer, Quin released her arms and they set about dressing in the clothes they had discarded earlier. A sharp sense of disappointment made him wonder if he was fighting a battle that couldn't be won. Her response had not been hopeful. Not even particularly interested.

The silence in the room felt oppressive. It triggered the memory of other silences just before she left him five years ago. They meant an inner withdrawal from him, a retreat to a personal space he couldn't touch, let alone share. He wanted to break into it, reach out to her, drag her back to him, but he realised force was not going to get him where he wanted to be.

For thirteen nights he'd ruled on what he and Nicole did or did not do together. She had been compliant, keeping to the deal, but here they were at the halfway mark, and Quin doubted any progress had been made towards his end goal—keeping her as his life partner.

He called down to reception and ordered his car to be brought up from the parking lot. As he was putting the telephone down, Nicole broke her silence. "Please ask for a taxi to be called, too."

She was brushing her hair, not looking at him.

"I'll drive you home," Quin said decisively.

"That's not necessary."

"It's the middle of the night," he argued. "I'll see you safely home, Nicole."

"What if I don't want you to?"

"Then you'll just have to suffer it because I'm not going to see you off in a taxi as though you were my whore," Quin retorted in exasperation with her determination to stay independent.

No reply to that.

She put her hairbrush back in her handbag and headed for the door. As Quin escorted her out of the hotel room to an elevator, the sobering thought hit him that he was going to fail if he didn't change what was wrong for her.

Their relationship had always been handled *his way*.

Somehow he had to turn that around.

But not on the point of driving her home.

"What time suits you for me to come tomorrow?" he asked as they rode the elevator down to the lobby.

Her head was lowered, the long silky curtain of her hair almost hiding her face. She didn't look up to answer him. "Zoe will be worn-out with excitement if you don't come in the morning," she said dryly. "Nine o'clock would probably be best. Ten at the latest."

"You can tell her I'll be there at nine."

"Don't forget the silver chain."

"I won't."

She nodded, not so much as glancing at him.

Quin could feel his jaw tightening, his hands clenching. He had to battle the instinct to fight. There was no physical conflict between him and Nicole. It was mental, emotional, and laying out his side of the past tonight was not enough to remove the hurt of being consigned to a secondary role in his life. She might very well be thinking that their daughter now had first place. He hadn't brought up marriage before meeting Zoe.

Bad timing.

It had always been bad timing with Nicole.

He needed to make a new plan to win her over.

His car was waiting at the entrance to the hotel lobby. The doorman ushered them over to it and opened the passenger side for Nicole to get in. She stepped forward quickly, lowering herself onto the seat and fastening her safety belt, keeping her head averted from Quin.

Tomorrow is another day, he told himself, reining in his frustration with the current situation as the doorman closed Nicole into the car and he rounded the bonnet to take the driver's seat. He started the engine, but before accelerating away from the hotel he shot a glance at Nicole, wanting to catch her looking at him. She wasn't. Her thick lashes were lowered but they couldn't quite catch the tears that were trickling through them, making shiny wet tracks down her cheeks.

Shock ripped through Quin.

In all the time he'd known her he'd never seen her in tears, and the certain knowledge that he must have caused them appalled him.

What had he said to give her grief?

What had he done?

His mind was in absolute tumult as he automatically manoeuvred the Audi back onto the route to Burwood. It was impossible to shake the image of Nicole sitting miserably alone, sad and defeated by forces that were beyond her control—forces that made her feel terribly vulnerable—no way out because he was Zoe's father.

There was no use arguing he didn't want to hurt her. He had in the past. A promise that it would be different this time probably sounded like empty words to her. Why should she believe it, given her past experience with him when he'd concentrated solely on his needs?

Words were useless.

Taking her to bed with him was useless, too. That was the same as before.

The thirteenth night…

He had to change what was happening on their nights together, show Nicole it was different. He could arrange a dinner party, invite not just his friends but hers, too, like the couple he'd met at the Havana Club, Jade and Jules Zilic. Involving other people might get Nicole to relax more in his company, and drawing her into his social circle would prove he wanted her by his side for more than just sex—his woman—*his wife!*

He heard a siren wailing and immediately checked his speedometer, aware that he hadn't done so and they'd been on Parramatta Road for some time without much traffic to slow them down. It was all right. He wasn't driving above the speed limit. He hadn't drunk any alcohol, either. Maybe the siren came from an ambulance on its way to an emergency.

If that were the case, he might have to pull

over into another traffic lane. The rear-vision mirror didn't show any vehicle with flashing lights yet the siren was definitely louder now, probably coming from a nearby street. He thought of Zoe, seriously ill with meningitis. Had she been rushed to hospital by ambulance in the middle of the night? He should have been at her side. At Nicole's side, as well.

It didn't occur to him to stop at the next intersection. The lights were green. There were cars in front of him, cars behind him. He was thinking of the daughter he hadn't known about, the years he'd lost, the years ahead of him and how he wanted to spend them.

He didn't see the car that hurtled straight past the red lights, speeding straight across the intersection towards him until it was too late to take evasive action. There was a split second when he knew it was going to crash into the Audi. Then the impact came and he lost consciousness.

CHAPTER FIFTEEN

PAIN.

Nicole struggled against sickening waves of it, a sense of urgency driving her to keep on fighting them, make it through. There was something she had to remember but her head was swimming in a whirlpool and it couldn't reach the important thing that hovered on the edge. She felt wetness on her face. Panic clutched her heart. Was she drowning?

Her eyes flew open and were hit by a swarm of dots.

Not water.

"Ah! You're awake," someone said.

The dots gradually grouped themselves into an image—a woman, dipping a cloth into a bowl on a tray.

"I'm just cleaning up your scalp wound which bled a lot," the woman said, gently applying a damp cloth to Nicole's head.

"Going to need quite a few stitches. We'll have to shave the hair around it, I'm afraid. But it will just be a strip. You've got so much hair, you'll have no problem covering it over."

Scalp wound...

She tried to speak, to ask what had happened, but all she could produce was a croak. Her throat was horribly dry.

"Want a piece of ice to suck?" the woman asked. Without waiting for an answer, she grabbed a paper cup from the tray and popped a small piece of ice into Nicole's mouth. "Better not drink a lot of water right now. You'll be going up for X-rays soon."

She must be in a hospital. And apparently there was uncertainty about the extent of her injuries if she had to have X-rays. The pain in her head made her wonder if she had a skull fracture.

Having worked some moisture off the piece of ice, Nicole managed to ask, "How... why...?"

"You've been in a car accident, dear," she was calmly informed.

A car accident meant she'd been in a car. Travelling where? For what reason?

She tried to concentrate her mind, clear

the thick fog. Gradually memories seeped through—the argument in the hotel, Quin insisting on driving her home, the anguish of wanting to believe they could have a good future together, the conflict of how he had made her feel in the past still churning through her. She remembered sitting in the car, silently fighting the tears welling from the torment in her heart, but she could find no memory at all of the car crashing—where it happened, why it happened, *what had happened to Quin.*

Alarm crashed around her head, making it feel like a bomb about to explode. Quin would be here with her if he could be. He'd feel responsible. No way would he leave her side until he was assured she was all right.

Her hand automatically lifted and clutched the arm of the nurse who was lifting the wet cloth to her head again. She needed her attention. Her full attention. The action startled the woman into looking directly at her.

"Quin…was he hurt, too?"

"Who, dear?"

"Quin Sola. He was with me. The driver of the car."

The nurse shook her head. "I don't know. He's not in this ward."

"What ward? Where am I?"

"The emergency ward at St. Vincent's Hospital. It's in Darlinghurst near the inner city."

"What time is it?"

The nurse checked her watch. "Almost two-thirty in the morning."

They'd left the hotel at about midnight. Not so very long ago. Nicole's chest felt so tight, she had difficulty finding enough breath to speak. "Quin would have stayed with me if he wasn't hurt. They would have brought him here, too, wouldn't they?" she demanded, her mind instinctively shying away from the dreadful possibility he might be dead.

"I'm sorry. I know nothing about him."

"Can't you find out for me?"

"A doctor will see you shortly," the nurse answered evasively. "You can ask him about your friend." And having resolved the matter to her satisfaction, she calmly removed Nicole's clasp on her arm, laid her hand back on the bed, patted it reassuringly, and went back to dabbing away at the scalp wound.

Full-blown panic swirled through Nicole, making her headache much worse. Her whole body ached. Finally she burst out,

"He's not my friend. He's the father of my daughter. And…and we're getting married."

That made her almost next of kin. She had a right to know what had happened to him. *What was happening.* He couldn't have been killed. Not Quin. He was the ultimate fighter. A winner, not a loser.

She clutched the nurse's arm again, her fingers digging in with the ferocity of feeling racing through her. "Stop that right now!"

Frowning, the nurse started to chide, "You mustn't…"

"I need to know about Quin. Go and call the admissions desk. Ask about him."

"I'm not supposed to…"

"I'll fight you until you do," Nicole threatened, totally uncaring of hospital protocol. "His name is Joaquin Sola. Have you got that?"

"Yes."

Nicole released her arm. The nurse set down the cloth on the mobile tray and hurried away. The effort of fighting for action had exhausted Nicole. Her head spun sickeningly. She closed her eyes and grimly held back a wave of nausea. How long she lay there, waiting for news, determined to remain conscious, she didn't know.

She kept willing Quin to be alive. For all she had railed against his intrusion on the life she'd made without him, and the terrible turmoil he'd given her over how good a father he'd be to Zoe, she couldn't bear the thought of never seeing him again, never being with him again. In her heart, she desperately wanted the chance for a different relationship to grow between them. He'd promised it would. A new beginning…

"Miss Ashton?"

A male voice.

She opened her eyes.

The nurse was back, accompanied by a man who obviously had more authority. "I'm Dr. Jefferson," he said. "Your fiancé is in surgery. He has broken ribs, one of which punctured his lung. I can assure you he's in good hands."

In surgery.

Fear sucked the breath out of her lungs.

Her father had died in surgery.

Which was why her mother had frantically sought other ways of ridding Harry of his liver cancer.

You can't die, Quin, she thought fiercely. *I won't have you die on me.*

"Now we have to get you up to X-rays,

Miss Ashton," the doctor carried on. "It appears you're only suffering from concussion and deep bruising but we have to check. Do we have your co-operation?"

"Yes. Thank you."

She clung to the thought that Quin was in good hands while she was X-rayed and had her head-wound stitched up. He was very fit and healthy. Most people did live through surgery. Quin would surely recover. It was just a matter of time.

As soon as she could, she'd tell him they could start planning to get married. The plain truth was she didn't want to live her life without him again. Pain or pleasure…she no longer cared…as long as they were making a future together as best they could. For Zoe. And for each other.

She gratefully accepted the sedation the doctor ordered. She needed the pain to go away, needed the gnawing treadmill of worries and resolutions to stop for a while, needed to blot out the waiting time before she could go and see Quin for herself. The last hazy thought drifting through her mind was…

Tomorrow will be a new day.
No looking back…only looking forward.

CHAPTER SIXTEEN

QUIN could hear his mother talking to him in Spanish. She was telling him about the games she'd played with Zoe, what an imaginative child she was, how sweet and caring and clever. It struck Quin there was something wrong with this scenario and he struggled to work out what it was. His mind seemed to have acquired layers of cotton wool. He concentrated on peeling them away. His mother continued to rave on about her beautiful grand-daughter.

But you've only seen photos of her, Quin suddenly thought, and the jab of that memory opened the door to other memories. The car accident. Nicole unconscious, bleeding from her head. His eyes flew open. He was in hospital, tubes attached to him, his mother sitting by his bed.

"Madre!" he croaked. His vocal chords felt as though they were rusty from disuse.

Before he could manage to say more, his mother leapt up from her chair in shock and alarm. "You are awake! *Gracias Dios!*" she cried as though it were a miracle, clasping her hands together in prayer. "I beg you, Joaquin, do not move. I must fetch a doctor."

She was already turning to do so when he got out the most important word. "Nicole…"

It halted her only momentarily. "Nicole is fine," she threw back at him in an agitated rush. "They only kept her here two nights to watch over her concussion and ensure there was no infection in the head wound. She has been home for days. Now please lie still while I get the doctor."

For days?

Relief at being assured of Nicole's well-being mixed with confusion over what had happened to him. How long had he been out of it? The tubes suggested they had been feeding him intravenously. He was attached to some kind of monitors, as well. He wriggled his toes to check that he still had mobility. His chest was sore. He had a hazy memory of being prepared for surgery.

But everything was okay. Nicole had not been badly hurt and he was alive, though not exactly kicking at the moment. His mother returned with a doctor and he was subjected to a series of medical checks, as well as a host of questions testing his memory and cognitive ability. Apparently he'd been in a comatose state since the surgery—broken ribs, punctured lung—but he was mending very nicely due to the absolute rest of not being conscious for the past five days.

Orderlies came in and cranked up the back third of the hospital bed so he could sit up with comfort and support. In moving, Quin caught sight of the blue Ulysses butterfly on top of the bedside cabinet. Seeing it caused a severe jolt to his heart. What did it mean? He hadn't forgotten the silver chain. Being injured through no fault of his own didn't deserve rejection.

He reached out to it. "How did this get here?"

"Zoe insisted on bringing it to make you feel better," his mother answered with an indulgent smile.

The surge of fighting adrenalin eased.

"Your daughter and fiancée have been regular visitors," the doctor remarked.

Fiancée?

Another thump to his heart.

"Oh!" His mother cried, clasping her

hands again. "I have to call Nicole. I promised I would if you woke up."

"Then do it, *Madre*," Quin urged, wanting very much to ascertain if Nicole had changed her mind about not marrying him. It was highly encouraging news that she had come to visit him in hospital, bringing Zoe with her, too! Or had she simply been obliging Zoe's wish to see her Daddy since he'd been in no condition to visit her. She might have simply called herself his fiancée to get easy access to him. Quin couldn't quite bring himself to believe she'd had a complete change of heart since Friday night.

The doctor told the orderlies to bring Quin a light meal, then took his leave, satisfied that his patient had come out of his coma with no ill effects.

His mother returned in a flurry of excitement. "I couldn't get onto Nicole. I forgot about evening classes at the dance school. But I spoke to Linda and she'll let Nicole know. I expect she'll come and visit you tomorrow morning, Joaquin."

Would she? Now that he was out of the woods?

"Is it evening?" he asked, the artificially lit room making it impossible to tell.

"Yes, dear, and Nicole won't get home until ten-thirty. Too late to visit tonight."

"You've met her mother, as well as Zoe?"

"Oh, yes. The police informed us separately of the accident—how they'd been chasing a car thief and he ran the red lights, ploughing straight into your car. We both rushed here to the hospital and introduced ourselves to each other in the waiting room. I must say Linda has been very kind, giving me her company and welcoming me into her home to visit Zoe."

"Did Nicole welcome you, too?"

She hesitated, possibly hearing the doubt in his voice. "She did not object, Joaquin," came the cautious reply. "Nicole has been very quiet. Mostly we've met in passing. We have taken turns to sit with you, trying to talk you out of the coma."

But he had not woken to Nicole's voice.

Had she talked to him?

If so, what had she said?

He looked at the blue butterfly—his gift returned to him.

Or was it at the heart of a circle linking Nicole and Zoe and himself for the rest of their lives?

He wouldn't know until Nicole came to see him…if she did.

* * *

Nicole stood outside the private room Quin had been moved to this morning and took several deep breaths, trying to calm the host of fluttering butterflies that had invaded her stomach. Evita Gallardo had assured her Quin was fine, completely himself again, and his first concern on waking from the coma had been to ask about her. So that had to mean he cared about her, didn't it? Cared deeply?

Or maybe he'd just remembered the accident and wanted to know if she'd survived it. After all, there was Zoe to consider. She was the mother of his child and it wouldn't be good for their daughter to be motherless.

Not good to be fatherless, either.

Zoe talked of little else but *her daddy*, her innocent little heart completely captivated by Quin. She'd been dancing around the house all morning unable to contain her joy and excitement at hearing he was better, sure in her own mind that the Ulysses butterfly had worked its magic on him.

Nicole knew she'd kept her own heart tightly guarded from the moment Quin had appeared in her life again, determined on hauling her back into his. She'd kept reminding herself of how it had been before, refusing to believe it could be any different this time around.

People didn't change.

But circumstances did.

Quin was now ready for the commitment of marriage and fatherhood. It was what she had once wanted from him. And the past few days of dreadful uncertainty had made her face the fact there was only ever going to be one man for her and he was lying behind this door, alive and well enough to make a future with her.

She didn't have to lay her heart open to him.

She just had to go in and say she'd decided to marry him.

Quin would take it from there.

All that would be required of her was to keep saying, *yes*, give him his own way and let it happen, ignore any pain and take the pleasure.

Her heart was pounding.

She took another deep breath and opened the door.

Waiting for Nicole to come had sharpened all Quin's senses. The click of the door opening was like a clash of cymbals in his ears. He felt his heart kick into overdrive as she stepped into his room, the instant impact of her unique beauty hitting him straight in the eye—a vision of such intense pleasure, all the magic moments she had ever given him streamed through his mind.

In one way it was like the very first time he'd seen her in the bank where they had both been employed seven years ago—the stunning sensuality of her long dark curly hair, swishing silkily around her lovely face; the thickly lashed green eyes, lit with a sharp intelligence that invariably challenged the man he was; the perfectly curved full-lipped mouth that promised so much sensual passion; the marvellous femininity of her entire body calling to everything male in him.

His woman…

He'd known it then. He knew it now. He'd let her go five years ago but he'd never succeeded in blocking her out of his memory, never succeeded in supplanting her with another woman, never felt so brilliantly alive with anyone else. He wanted her. He needed her. He had to have her.

A flush brightened her cheeks. Was he discomforting her with his staring? Did she feel the strength of the desire pouring from him?

"Hi!" he said, trying to sound normal, flashing a warm smile to welcome her into his life again.

"Hi!" she echoed, returning a curiously shy little smile as though she felt awkward with the situation. "I'm glad you're back with us, Quin," she added, her eyes eloquently expressing relief at his recovery.

With us. Not *with me.*

But she hadn't wished him dead, hadn't wished him completely out of her life. And she wasn't wearing jeans today, either. In place of her usual uniform for carrying out her deal with him, she wore a clingy green top outlining her lovely full breasts and a swinging frilled skirt in green and orange and brown—strappy orange sandals on her feet. Did this mean she felt differently about their relationship?

"I'm glad to see you looking so…so well," he replied, his mind quickly skipping any words she might not want to hear from him. It was important not to make her feel pressured, he remembered, but he couldn't stop himself from asking, "Please…will you sit with me for a while, Nicole?"

"I want to talk to you," she said with an air

of resolution, moving forward to take the chair beside his bed.

Perfume wafted into his nostrils. Quin breathed in the wonderfully exotic scent—the sweet smell of hope. Surely no woman wore perfume for a man she wasn't interested in, but he warned himself not to assume too much. Casting around for a safe topic, he smiled whimsically and said, "The blue butterfly has been keeping me company. Please thank Zoe for it."

The green eyes met his directly. "I promised to bring her in to visit you this afternoon, so you can thank her yourself, Quin. She'd like that. I needed to speak to you first, get things straight between us."

Tension streaked through him. His mind pulsed with the certainty she was about to recant the title of his fiancée. Everything within him moved to battle-readiness and it took an enormous effort of will to remain still and silent and simply wait for her to lay out her position.

Her lashes swept down. She took a deep breath, clearly gathering herself to speak. Then her gaze lifted and locked onto his and the windows to her soul reflected a desperate need to make everything right.

"I was wrong to be so mean-hearted towards you, Quin," she rushed out. "Using your…your desire for me to make you pay debts that had nothing to do with you."

"I hurt you with my obsessive pursuit of the money my father took," he said quietly. "Do you think I don't understand that, Nicole?"

"You had good reason to do what you did," she argued.

"I sacrificed *us* to a boyhood trauma."

"Your mother held you to it, Quin."

"No it was me, too. My pride. Worth too little in the end," he said with a rueful grimace. "I don't know if you can forgive me that, Nicole…"

"Yes, I can. I will," she asserted emphatically, then hesitated, her expression flicking to eloquent appeal. "If you can forgive me for keeping Zoe to myself."

"My fault for not sharing with you."

"No. What I did was wrong. It was mean and nasty and vengeful. And I'm sorry…sorry…" She shook her head fretfully. "You gave your mother back her life. You gave *my* mother back her life. And all I've done is bitterly condemn you for not…not…" Tears welled and she quickly veiled them, looking down at her lap where her hands held each other tightly. Keeping her courage screwed to the sticking point?

"Not giving what we had together enough value," he finished for her. "I should have, Nicole," he added gravely. "I didn't realise until after it was gone how much I should have valued it. I've been trying to show you…"

"I don't want to talk about that," she choked out, then took another deep breath and lifted her chin, wet eyes defiantly open to meet his. "It was a different time and place, Quin. This is now. You said on Friday night that you wanted me to be your wife."

His lungs stopped working. His chest hurt. His heart drummed in his ears. He worked hard at forcing up enough breath to say, "I do," desperately hoping this confirmation wouldn't draw another rejection.

"Okay. I've decided to marry you. Zoe should have her father on hand and I—" she swallowed hard "—I want to be with you, too."

Relief surged through him, easing the pain caused by tension. Elation danced through his mind. He smiled. "We belong together, Nicole."

"Yes," she agreed.

But there was no answering smile, no joy in her eyes.

"Nothing like a crisis to bring people together," he said ironically.

"Yes," she agreed, echoing his irony.

At least it wasn't loaded with bitterness, Quin thought, though he was acutely aware that she wasn't professing any love for him. Maybe that was forever lost. He was sensing only a recognition and an acceptance that they had a strong enough personal connection to make a marriage work, given that their daughter's best interests should be considered.

A heavy weight settled on his heart. He'd done this to Nicole, failing to meet her emotional needs in the past, draining her of the love she had given him. Forgiveness for his failure didn't guarantee restoration of what they'd once had together. It just meant moving on, leaving the bad emotional baggage behind, and her love for Zoe was probably a prime mover in her decision to marry him.

"What happened to the photo albums?" he asked, suddenly recalling they'd been in the car—precious mementoes of Zoe's life so far.

"They weren't damaged," Nicole quickly

assured him. "They were recovered by the police and handed over to my mother."

"Well, thank God they weren't lost," he muttered, closing his eyes as a sickening wave of weakness rolled through him. The coma might have been good for healing after surgery but the days of immobility had sapped his body of its normal strength, letting him know it when he least expected it, telling him now that the energy spent on this meeting with Nicole came at a cost.

Everything did. His determination to restore family honour had cost him Nicole's love, cost him four years of his daughter's life. Getting Nicole to connect with him again had cost him a lot of money. Not that he cared about that. He just wished he could have worked it all differently.

"Quin?"

He heard the quavery note of anxiety in her voice and savagely told himself that some measure of caring was still there and he could build on it. He felt her hand clutch his, enfolding it in warm softness, gently pressing. She didn't want to walk away from him. Not this time.

"Are you all right? Should I call a doctor?"

"No. Just feeling a bit faint. It passes."

"Maybe I should leave you to rest."

Her hand started releasing his. He grabbed it, holding onto her. She was his woman. She had to know it.

"I'll be back this afternoon with Zoe," she assured him.

He opened his eyes, shooting her a look of blazing need that was totally beyond his will to control. "Kiss me, Nicole. That will make me feel better."

It startled her, fear and uncertainty flicking across her face. He tugged her hand, pulling her towards him. She rose from the chair, stood beside the bed, her eyes worriedly searching his. "Are you sure, Quin?"

"Yes."

She bent and grazed her lips gently over his, her free hand resting on the pillow beside his head. Quin closed his eyes again, breathing in her scent, savouring the taste of her, wishing he could hold her close, ruefully accepting it would be unwise, given his present condition.

His tongue flicked out to tease her into kissing him more deeply. She responded, making a slow, sensual and very intimate assault on his mouth. Pleasure flowed through him. He was sure there was an edge of passion in the feelings she transmitted, her own need and want tightly restrained, yet tugging at her to re-affirm the decision she'd made to marry him, be with him for the rest of her life.

When she drew back, her face was flushed, her eyes glinting with worry again. "You're sure this is all right?"

"Yes. Thank you."

It was all right.

He felt the love was still there, set at a distance but still there.

One way or another, he'd close that distance.

Nicole wasn't going away.

She had agreed to marry him.

CHAPTER SEVENTEEN

HER wedding day—the day when she said the really big *yes* to Quin. The reality of it was all around her in this penthouse suite at the Intercontinental Hotel—her mother, Zoe and the bridesmaids all dressed ready to go to the ceremony. In another thirty minutes, a stretch limousine would be taking them to the venue. Three o'clock, Quin had said, and time was ticking away. Yet Nicole couldn't quite shake the feeling she was in a dream.

"What kind of wedding would you like?" Quin had asked.

"I don't know," she had answered truthfully. "What do you want?"

"Something beautiful, truly memorable…"

"Why don't you plan it, Quin?"

He'd frowned. "It's the bride's special day. I want you to be happy with it."

"Then make it special for me."

The challenge had tripped off her tongue, spurred by wanting to have some measure of how special the occasion was for him. Let him have his way. All his way. It might reveal quite a bit about how much *she* meant to him, too.

As Nicole sat still while the beautician moved around her, putting the last finishes to her bridal make-up, she couldn't help thinking that if one put a money value on this wedding and that was the measure of how special it was to Quin, then it was spectacularly special. On the other hand, she wasn't sure if he was putting on a show for her or for other people.

Her side of the guest list was relatively small. She had a few friends amongst the mothers of little girls at the dance school, and two of those were her bridesmaids, along with Jade. Her mother's friends in the world of dance were not exactly numerous, either. Quin's side not only carried a lot of people from the Sydney social set and important business clients, but quite a large contingent from Argentina—the Gallardo family and their close friends.

Not that it mattered, she told herself.

They were getting married.

That was the only really important thing.

"I've never seen you look so beautiful, Nicole," Jade remarked, a note of awe in her voice.

Amazing what cosmetics in skilled hands can do, she thought, smiling at her friend. "You, too. I really like that burnt copper shade of red for your hair."

Jade laughed. "Couldn't leave it purple. Since I'm chief bridesmaid, it might have distracted from the bride."

"Thanks for everything you've done, Jade. You and Jules. The dresses you designed and made are wonderful."

"Well, we did have instructions from Zoe and Quin," she said archly. "Got to say that guy has moved to a great address, Nic. Wherever he was in the past, what you have now is a man who's totally committed to giving his woman a wonderful wedding. Namely you."

Yes, he had moved, Nicole silently agreed. Certainly since he'd come out of hospital two months ago, he'd won over her mother with his kindness and consideration, bonded deeply with their daughter, and had set about introducing her to his friends, taking her out to dinners and shows, not concentrating their entire relationship on sex, which was still great, but no longer the only thing they shared.

"You do love him, don't you?" Jade asked softly.

"Yes," she answered unequivocally, looking down at the magnificent emerald and diamond engagement ring Quin had given her. *For better or for worse,* she thought, *as long as we both shall live.*

Zoe came dancing into the bedroom. "Is it time for your dress now, Mummy?" she asked excitedly.

"Yes," the beautician answered, satisfied with the result of her artistry.

"I love *your* dress, Zoe," Nicole said, thinking how well the deep blue suited her dark colouring.

She twirled to show it off. "It's the same blue as the Ulysses butterfly. I told Daddy that was what I wanted. And then we decided the bridesmaids should be like the Australian sky, light blue in the morning, bright blue in the middle of the day, and dark blue after sunset. Wasn't that a good idea, Mummy?"

"A lovely idea, Zoe," she agreed, and it had been transmitted by Jade and Jules into beautiful floor-length georgette gowns with the three shades of blue graduating down from the light colour for the strapless bodice to the deeper shades in the skirt.

"And Daddy had these butterfly clips in my hair made specially for me," Zoe declared proudly.

"They look very pretty."

As did the blue silk butterflies adorning the hair of the bridesmaids. Quin's idea, Jade had told her, to mark a very special day.

Her mother, dressed in a very elegant deep violet outfit to blend with the bridal party, made a brisk entrance. "It's twenty to three, Nicole. We're not going to be late, are we?" she asked anxiously.

"No, Mum. I'm all ready bar for the wedding gown, and as you can see, the dresser is taking it out of its plastic wrapping now."

The wedding planner Quin had hired, had staff running everywhere, ensuring everything was perfectly done; the hairdresser, the beautician, the dresser, the florist. Nothing was overlooked and each step of the preparation was on schedule.

The gown was unzipped and held out for Nicole to step into. She stood up and discarded the wrap-around she'd worn through most of the afternoon.

"Wow!" Zoe cried, her eyes popping at the sexy underwear.

Nicole gave a nervous laugh, hoping Quin would appreciate her own personal contribution to their wedding later tonight.

"Is that bride stuff, too, Mummy?"

"It sure is!" Jade answered, laughing at Zoe's innocent remark. "I just hope you're going to love the dress, Nic."

She'd never seen it. She'd been fitted for it with the underlining for the bodice, not once with the dress itself. A froth of white georgette was pooled on the floor. There seemed like many layers of it. Nicole stepped into the space at the centre of it, careful not to snag her high heels in the fabric. She fitted her arms through shoestring shoulder straps as the gown was pulled up her body. Then the dresser zipped it into place and Nicole stared at her reflection in the cheval mirror placed ready for her to see herself.

The bodice was tightly fitted from her breasts to her hips and intricately and beautifully beaded with tiny crystals creating the shape of a butterfly. There was a centre split in the front skirt to just above knee high for easy walking up any stairs, which might have been difficult with so many floating layers of georgette. At the back, the skirt fell gracefully into a train, making it very bridal.

Her mother heaved a happy sigh. "You look wonderful, Nicole."

"Spectacular!" Jade said with satisfaction. "Are you happy with it?"

"Yes. It's…it's stunning!" Nicole said dazedly. "Thank you so much."

"The concept came from Quin. Jules and I simply translated it as best we could."

Quin had gone to so much personal trouble to get everything right for her. Right in a very meaningful sense. Surely no man tried to please a woman so much if he didn't love her, but he'd never said the words. He would today, in the wedding ceremony. Would he mean them, or would he just be repeating the traditional marriage vows?

"Now your flowers," the dresser said, handing Nicole the three red roses she was to carry as her bouquet.

Not hot-house buds. These roses were in full bloom and strongly scented. As was the one that had been positioned in her hair, just above her left ear. Jade had told her Quin didn't want a bridal veil to be worn—nothing to hide her hair, just a red rose to enhance its natural beauty.

Red roses for love.

Please let it be true, she thought, her heart yearning for a fairy-tale ending to all she had been through with Quin.

The bridesmaids' bouquets were handed out, posies of roses in every colour. "Because butterflies like lots of pretty colours, Mummy," Zoe informed her.

Nicole's nerves were fluttering as they were all led down to the waiting limousines which would take them to the wedding venue—still a closely guarded secret.

It was another stunning surprise when they were driven only a short distance—to the Sydney Opera House!—and escorted up to the northern Concert Hall foyer which featured the fantastic arch of windows over-looking the harbour. Rows and rows of white-sheathed chairs had been placed on red carpet—all of them filled with wedding guests. White pedestals held spectacular ar-rangements of red roses. The whole scene was fantastic.

But Quin was no fantasy. He broke away from the standing line of groomsmen at the front, and looking heart-wrenchingly hand-some in his formal black dinner suit and snow-white dress shirt, he strode confidently down the make-shift aisle to claim her, his megawatt smile shining, telling her he was brilliantly alive.

"Happy?" he asked, his grey eyes smoking warmly with pleasure in her.

"Yes." She returned his smile, openly expressing her pleasure in him. "Very happy."

"Good! Today I'm trying to make up for all the romance I didn't give you, Nicole."

Romance…was that love?

"You truly are a star player, Quin. In this, as well as everything else," she said, feeling overwhelmed by all he done to make their wedding special for her—beautiful and very memorable.

"You count most of all," he murmured huskily, taking her arm and linking it around his.

Those words kept fizzing in Nicole's mind like a cocktail of joy as Quin walked her down the aisle to the marriage celebrant. Her mother and Zoe had already gone ahead to take their chairs in the front row. Her bridesmaids brought up the end of the little procession and lined up beside her as she and Quin halted beside his groomsmen.

The ceremony was short, but very emotional for Nicole. Both Tony Fisher, Quin's best man, and Jade delivered moving readings about love and marriage. Someone with a beautiful voice sang "All The Way." When Quin spoke his vows, his voice vibrated with deep feeling, bringing tears to her eyes. She only just managed to blink them away as they signed the marriage certificate, composing herself to meet the well-wishers who crowded around them afterwards.

The fabulous surprises weren't over.

They kept coming.

After leaving the Opera House, they boarded a luxurious catamaran and cruised the harbour. Wedding photographs were taken with the background of the great coat hanger bridge and a glorious sunset. French champagne flowed, gourmet canapés were served, and the guests partied happily, many wanting their photographs taken with the bride and groom.

Quin's elderly but still very distinguished-looking grandfather, Juan Gallardo, welcomed Nicole into *the family,* congratulated his grandson on acquiring such a beautiful wife, and remarked that he could understand why Quin had decided to make Sydney his home. Even Buenos Aires could not outshine such a splendid city. And, of course, since the woman of his heart was Australian…yes, he understood…but Joaquin must bring Nicole to Argentina for a visit sometime in the near future.

Quin's mother had a lovely time, busily showing off Zoe to all her Gallardo relatives. "My grand-daughter…" she kept saying proudly.

Nicole was pleased to see her own mother mingling happily with her old associates from dancing competitions, no doubt catching up on all the professional gossip and swapping stories about especially talented dance pupils coming up. It was good to know she was really getting back to normal, interested in business and people again. Even better, that she seemed to have picked up an admirer who was dancing attendance on her.

There was nothing Nicole could do about the empty nest syndrome. She and Zoe would be moving in with Quin after the honeymoon and her mother would be alone in the Burwood house. At least running the dance school should keep her occupied most of the time and they'd meet there several days a week. They weren't dropping out of her life.

The catamaran docked at Mosman, almost directly across the water from the Opera House and they were transported to another mystery location—the landmark Taronga Centre at the Taronga Zoo, once again overlooking Sydney Harbour.

The reception room was decked out in traditional white linen with red roses on all the tables. They feasted on Sydney rock oysters, Tasmanian salmon and chocolate coated strawberries with King Island cream, and were entertained by a live band backing a great singer. A three-tier wedding cake—a decorator's wonderful work of art—waited to be cut. Before that happened, however, came the speeches.

Tony Fisher stood up and soon had the guests laughing with his charm and wit, finally declaring that only his good friend, Quin, could have danced the elusive and lovely Nicole off her feet and into wedlock. He called for a toast to the bride and groom, which was heartily raised and drunk.

Quin rose from his chair.

Nicole held her breath, her heart hammering her chest. He'd made their wedding day unbelievably special—the ultimate peak of romance. Would he top it now with what she most wanted to hear?

"Earlier this evening my grandfather, Juan Gallardo—" he gestured to the table where the old man sat "—rightly recognised Nicole as the woman of my heart." He turned and smiled at her, and her own heart stopped its wild pounding and flooded with pleasure. She even started breathing again as he resumed his speech to the guests.

"When I first met Nicole seven years ago, what instantly flashed through my mind was…this is my woman. Fortunately the desire for us to be together was mutual and she did become my woman. She filled that role, giving me her love for two years, but I made the huge mistake of not really appreci-ating how big a gift that was. I didn't share my heart with her and I made her feel as though she was no more than a possession which I picked up and put down at my con-venience. So I lost her…"

The sadness and regret in his voice was poignant and the dead silence in the room re-spected his feelings. Nicole was stunned that he was revealing so much and found herself flushing at his use of the bitter accusations she had thrown at him.

"I not only lost my woman, but I also lost the child she bore me—our beautiful daughter, Zoe—who has known from her mother all the love I didn't value enough."

Her stomach contracted at the acknowledgment that she had loved him. Did he know she still did?

"Five years passed before our paths crossed again, more than long enough for me to know how empty all my achievements were without her at my side. I would have done anything to win her back and this was where Fate smiled kindly on me. Nicole needed help and I could give it. Which earned me time with her. Time enough to demonstrate I would not repeat the mistakes of the past."

He was humbling himself in front of all these people, humbling himself to atone for the hurt he'd inflicted. Nicole would not have asked it of him. Yet she was totally captivated by the deeply personal confession.

"I learnt the importance of sharing. I learnt that open communication is the cornerstone for trust and understanding. I learnt that the gift of love is infinitely precious and must

always be nurtured and cherished, never ne-
glected."

He paused, then fervently added, "I hope
I can carry these lessons into the future that
Nicole has granted me in becoming my wife
today. I certainly aim to because I don't want
her to ever doubt how very much I do love
her and will always love her."

There it was! He'd said it! And there
wasn't a skerrick of doubt in her mind about
it as he turned to her once more, smiling his
love, shining it straight into her eyes, her
soul.

"Nicole is more than the woman of my
heart. She is the Queen of my heart," he
stated emphatically, then held out his hand
to her. "Will you do me the honour of
dancing with me, my love?"

An incandescent happiness was bursting
through her. "Yes," spilled joyfully from her
lips as she took his hand and rose from her
chair, wanting to be taken into his embrace,
feel him close to her, pour out her own love
for him.

All the guests stood up from their tables,
wildly applauding them as Quin led her onto
the small dance floor. The band began
playing the sentimental evergreen tune of

Moon River—and she and Quin were together again—truly, deeply together—as they waltzed around the floor in perfect unison, every step a harmony of the heart.

They were not aware of being watched by all the guests wearing benevolent smiles, some of them wiping emotional tears from their eyes. They were only aware of each other—the strong sexual chemistry they'd always had, now enhanced by the magical feeling of so much more bonding them for the rest of their lives.

"I love you, too, Quin," she whispered, her eyes openly avowing what she had kept hidden in her heart, frightened of having it crushed again.

The fear was gone.

Quin had demolished it.

"Thank you for such a perfect day," she added, loving him all the more for giving it to her.

"*You* make it so," he murmured.

"I'll treasure it in my memory for as long as I live."

"We'll build a treasure house of beautiful memories, Nicole."

She smiled. "Like our very own butterfly tree."

He smiled back. "Yes. Our very own."

They danced on to the music of love in their hearts, knowing they would *always* dance together because the love would last forever.

HARLEQUIN®
Presents

The world's bestselling romance series...
The series that brings you your favorite authors,
month after month:

Helen Bianchin...Emma Darcy
Lynne Graham...Penny Jordan
Miranda Lee...Sandra Marton
Anne Mather...Carole Mortimer
Susan Napier...Michelle Reid

and many more uniquely talented authors!

Wealthy, powerful, gorgeous men...
Women who have feelings just like your own...
The stories you love, set in exotic, glamorous locations...

HARLEQUIN®
Presents

Seduction and Passion Guaranteed!

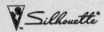

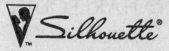

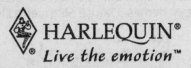

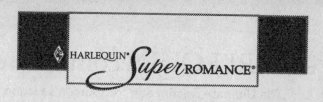
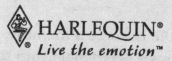

eHARLEQUIN.com

The Ultimate Destination for Women's Fiction

Visit eHarlequin.com's Bookstore today
for today's most popular books at great prices.

- An extensive selection of romance books by top authors!

- Choose our convenient "bill me" option. No credit card required.

- New releases, Themed Collections and hard-to-find backlist.

- A sneak peek at upcoming books.

- Check out book excerpts, book summaries and Reader Recommendations from other members and post your own too.

- Find out what everybody's reading in Bestsellers.

- Save BIG with everyday discounts and exclusive online offers!

- Our Category Legend will help you select reading that's exactly right for you!

- Visit our Bargain Outlet often for huge savings and special offers!

- Sweepstakes offers. Enter for your chance to win special prizes, autographed books and more.

Your purchases are 100% guaranteed—so shop online at www.eHarlequin.com today!

INTBB104R